Metamorphosis

Metamorphosis

and other stories

Franz Kafka

Translated by Richard Stokes

ET REMOTISSIMA PROPE

100 PAGES

100 PAGES

Published by Hesperus Press Limited

4 Rickett Street, London SW6 1RU

www.hesperuspress.com

First published by Hesperus Press Limited, 2002

Introduction and English language translation © Richard Stokes, 2002
Foreword © Martin Jarvis, 2002

Designed and typeset by Fraser Muggeridge
Printed in the United Arab Emirates by Oriental Press

ISBN: 1-84391-014-4

CONTENTS

There are many interpretations of Kafka's *Metamorphosis*. Choose a scholar, take your choice.

My own work as a performer, producer and would-be interpreter of stories teaches me to ask, first, 'is it true?' That doesn't mean, of course, 'did a young travelling salesman *really* wake one morning to find himself "transformed in his bed into a monstrous insect"?' We've read the Brothers Grimm, we've heard *The Cunning Little Vixen*, and may even have caught a production of Capek's *The Insect Play*. We know our European allegories.

Next question: 'Does this text speak to me?' Answer: 'Loud and clear.' To you too, I hope. It may say something different to each of us. *Metamorphosis* is a work of genius. I believe wholeheartedly in Gregor Samsa's plight, in every desperate action of his father and mother and sister. I acknowledge the human truth of the extraordinary events that take place in the Samsa household.

Why does Franz Kafka's masterpiece speak to me? After all, unlike Kafka, I neither grew up in Prague nor am I Jewish, nor was I, unlike Gregor, ever a young salesman doing his best to support an impoverished family. No, but like all major works of art, the resonance feeds back to fundamental things in myself. Nothing very remarkable: I was brought up in south London in the fifties. I had a father, mother and sister. Still have all three. Like most of us, I have sampled the ups and downs, the embarrassments and puzzles and fears of family life. Gregor Samsa's horrifying adventure provokes startling memories. Like him I have received visits from disappointed and puzzled authority, been threatened with the doctor, even an emergency locksmith. I've stayed in bed rather than face the world and, amazingly, managed to persuade Dr Murphy that I was too unwell to leave the confines of my room. All right, I wasn't a young man of twenty or so, living in a certain political and ethnic isolation. I was nine, fearful to start a new school term where I would be confronted by the monsters of algebra and Latin. Nevertheless, I remained, like Gregor, under the covers, nursing this self-imposed illness, later creeping out onto the tiny landing in my pyjamas and ear-wigging the rest of the family as they applauded my sister playing her latest exercises on the descant recorder. Had I heard of Gregor at that time I would surely have sympathised with his sense of detachment as he crept nearer to listen to his own sister: 'the sound of violin-playing came from the kitchen.' Me and poor old Greg – two of a kind. It goes further. One evening I suffered the ignominy of a visit from my form-master, Mr Merrit, who called to check up on me. He was returning my arithmetic test (low marks) and I heard him ask, like Kafka's equally investigative chief clerk, 'He isn't trying to make fools of us, is he?' Gregor's internal anguish tangles with mine: why on earth was I condemned to go to a school 'where the slightest lapse promptly aroused the greatest suspicion'? 'Your achievements have recently been most unsatisfactory' we were both told. Melancholy and a 'faint dull ache' were shared experiences.

A few years on I endured the weird indignity of locking myself in the lavatory and the key getting jammed. 'Come on, Martin, stick at it, harder, work on that lock!' cry my parents and sister. (You'd think they must have read Kafka.) 'Get a locksmith immediately,' cries Gregor's father – and mine. In fact Gregor was spared Mr Rowe the plumber being summoned with his tool-box to the rescue. I still replay in my head the Kafkaesque humiliation of waiting a whole half hour while he wrenched and wrestled with spanners and screwdrivers. 'Martin! Martin!' chivvied my family, all three dancing up and down wanting to go to the loo, until he was forced to take the door off its hinges. Immediately I beetled through the open gap, across the landing and into my bedroom, hurling myself, sobbing, onto the bed in an agony of shame. ' "Gregor!" came the soft plaintive voice of his sister'; 'Martin? Aren't you well? Is there anything you want?' The two lads become one for a moment in my mind.

Why behave so oddly? Fear? Insecurity? Incipient madness? Some say the story is actually an account of deep-seated mental illness. I leave it you. Why did Kafka deconstruct his hero into an insect? I leave that to you, too.

A central theme, both in *Metamorphosis* and in the shorter story *The Sentence*, is the uneasy relationship between father and son, their mutual non-communication. Can I relate to that? You bet. When I was roughly Gregor's age Dad lent me his precious Hillman Minx so I could drive a girlfriend home in style. On my return I motored straight into the garage, and jammed my foot not on the brake but on the accelerator. The car leapt straight into the rear wall. I sat, like Gregor with the apple lodged in his back, slumped over the wheel, bruised and with my 'senses in a complete blur'. My parents' bedroom was directly above. It was my mother who came hurrying downstairs in her dressing-gown. As soon as she saw I wasn't dead I was dispatched to my room. 'Frightened of making his father impatient' – that's me and my alter ego in tandem again – I somehow managed for the next three weeks, though living in the same house, to avoid seeing Dad at all. I would crouch like a nervous bug, antennae at the ready, until he'd gone to the office. Then, cautiously, emerge.

You may perceive as you read *Metamorphosis* that every

character, not just Gregor, becomes transformed in some way. We all change, as life goes on and, if we're luckier than the Samsas, we may just morph into newer, better models. I'm a dad myself and am continually concerned about my two boys. When crossing a busy street with them I instinctually spread my arms in an age-old protective gesture against possible oncoming traffic. They smile indulgently – one is a cool thirty-six-year-old composer of music, the other a thirty-four-year-old barrister. But my young grandchild grasps my hand voluntarily. She is still to grow up. And transform.

Franz Kafka's vision isn't as sunny as my own currently idyllic family picture. He reaches out from an uncertain past to remind us of ourselves, perhaps to warn us of our possibilities, good and ill. Using a deceptively lighter mood in the brilliant eleven-line anecdote *Give Up*, he suggests that none of us really knows the road on which we travel.

Great art speaks to us all, in entirely personal ways. There is a dazzling mystery at the heart of *Metamorphosis* that will forever defy academia's efforts to nail its meaning absolutely. It is enough for us to recognise its ultimate humanity and – like Gregor, like Kafka, like us all – continue to crawl forward, sometimes fearfully, on our little legs, in the dark.

– Martin Jarvis, 2002

INTRODUCTION

Franz Kafka was born in Prague in 1883 of Jewish parents with whom he lived for almost his entire life. He was the oldest of six children – two boys died in infancy, and three girls were murdered by the Nazis in the early 1940s. His mother Julie, née Löwy, was the daughter of a prosperous brewer, and Kafka felt a spiritual affinity with the rabbis and Talmudists among her forebears. His father, Hermann, was a successful businessman who had no time for his son's intellectual and literary interests, and insisted on his studying law at university. Kafka completed his studies in 1906, and two years later took up an appointment with an insurance company in Prague. Although he worked in insurance all his life, and rose to a position of considerable authority before being pensioned in 1922, he always resented the time it took away from his writing. He usually wrote at night, sometimes through the night, thus working himself into a state of exhaustion that must have contributed to his early death. Tuberculosis of the larynx, which was diagnosed in 1917, caused him to leave the Workers' Accident Insurance Office, and in 1919 he sought a cure in various sanatoria. He spent the final stages of his illness in a nursing home at Kierling, near Vienna, and died on 3 June 1924, aged forty. He published little in his lifetime and gave instructions in his will that all his unpublished writings should be destroyed. Fortunately for posterity, this directive was ignored by his friend and executor Max Brod, who immediately after Kafka's death prepared both *The Trial* and *The Castle* for publication, in 1925 and 1926 respectively. Kafka himself only published a few shorter works in his lifetime: *Meditation* (1913), *The Stoker: A Fragment* (1913), *The Transformation* [*Metamorphosis*] (1915), *The Sentence* (1916),

A Country Doctor: Little Tales (1919) and *In the Penal Colony* (1919).

Kafka suffered throughout his life from a feeling of estrangement and inadequacy. Although he lived in Prague, he was German, and therefore cut off from the Czechs who formed the majority of the country's population. Being a Jew in Prague also caused identity problems, to such an extent that many of Kafka's friends and relatives distanced themselves from Judaism in an attempt to become more fully assimilated in Czech society. The Czechs, however, tended to associate the Jews with the prosperous German minority in their midst; while that same German minority tended to perceive Jews as Jews – a race apart, despite their linguistic links. As an official in a workers' insurance company, he did not entirely belong to the middle-class; and as the son of a middle-class family, he did not entirely belong to the working-class either. Nor was his confidence boosted by being an artist in what was predominantly a business world.

This feeling of being an outsider would have mattered less if Kafka had found support within his family. As an infant, however, he saw very little of his mother; both his brothers died before he was six years old, and by the time he started school he was already identified as a child who was used to solitude. His father, probably unwittingly, filled him with a strong sense of inadequacy and guilt, and this was to become one of the themes of *The Trial*, *The Castle* and many of his shorter works of fiction. The obsessive nature of this unhappy relationship is evident from Kafka's lengthy *Letter to his Father* of 1919, which describes the neurotic father-son relationship, and which was neither sent nor published during his lifetime. There we learn (although we cannot be sure to what extent Kafka is creating myths about himself) how he was not allowed to introduce a topic of conversation; that he was forbidden to contradict; that his father never read aloud to him but taught him how to march and salute and sing military songs; how his mother, though she tried to defend her son, never did so forcefully; how Kafka lived in fear of his father's reddening face, whose braces were laid threateningly over the back of a chair. Two passages in particular highlight the appalling nature of their relationship and the way in which Kafka's father undermined his son's confidence and self-respect. When Kafka proudly presented him with a recently published book, his father ('who was usually playing cards when a book arrived') said dismissively: 'Legs auf den Nachttisch' ('Put in on the bedside table'). And when Kafka announced his wish to get engaged, his father gave the following cruel reply:

> 'She probably put on an exquisite blouse, as only Prague Jewesses know how to, whereupon you naturally decided to marry her. As quickly as possible, within a week, tomorrow, today. I don't understand you, you are an adult, you live in a town and yet insist on marrying the first woman who comes along. Is there no alternative? If you're afraid, I'll go with you.' [The father is, of course, referring to a brothel.]

A similar scene occurs in *The Sentence* when the father accuses the son of desecrating his mother's memory for being sexually aroused, as the father asserts, when his fiancée lifted her skirts. The story was written in the course of a single night (22/23 September 1912) and draws heavily upon Kafka's private experience. In his diary entry of 11 February 1913 he writes that the surname of the protagonist Georg Bende[mann] is linked to his own name (through the same disposition of consonants and vowels), and the name of Frieda Brandenfeld with that of his fiancée, Felice Bauer, to whom the story is in fact dedicated. Georg's father, like Kafka's perhaps, resents the fact that he is being supplanted (in business and in Georg's resolve to found his own family) and interprets his son's action of putting him to bed as a symbolic act of burial. Soon after completing the story, Kafka admitted that he had had Freud in mind while writing it – hardly surprising, since Georg's unexpressed wishes ('If only he'd fall and smash himself to pieces') illustrate so graphically what Freud wrote in *Das Tabu und die Ambivalenz der Gefühlsregungen* (*Taboo and Emotional Ambivalence*), namely that any emotional attachment to a particular person conceals hostility in the unconscious.

Although the theme of the father also plays a prominent part in *Metamorphosis*, Kafka's often symbolical and oblique style of writing has caused this and many other of his works to be interpreted in widely different ways. The American scholar Professor Stanley Corngold published a volume in 1973 called *The Commentators' Despair* which lists over one hundred and thirty interpretations of *Metamorphosis*. The work can be seen as: the struggle between father and son, whose metamorphosis represents a kind of self-punishment for his competitive striving against his father; a parable on human reactions to suffering and disease; a protest against the way in which industrialisation dehumanises human relationships; a punishment meted out to Gregor Samsa for leading an emotionally unfulfilled life. There have also been religious interpretations that view Gregor as a false messiah, and others that interpret Gregor's transformation as something positive and spiritually valuable. Throughout Kafka's diaries and letters there are continual references to his conviction that his work as a writer is incompatible with family life, marriage or his career as an insurance expert. 'He felt as if he were being shown the way to the unknown nourishment that he so craved', is the way that Kafka describes Gregor's reaction to his sister's violin-playing; it is as though true spiritual reality can only be achieved when he has assumed the shape of a verminous insect and rejected all materialistic values.

Isolation need not necessarily be seen as something entirely negative. To be on the outside can have advantages: it enables the poet or artist to observe with increased accuracy, and to gain greater insights. A diary entry of 19 October 1921 talks about the need for anyone who is unable to cope with life to have two hands free – one with which to fend off fate, and the other to record what he sees among the rubble, for 'he sees more than others and sees different things; although he is dead while alive, he is the real survivor.' Such is the position of the Hunter Gracchus. After a hunting accident 1,500 years ago, he has been condemned to a state of limbo between life and death, because his 'death ship' lost its way and now drifts along the waterways of the world. There is a sense in which, by belonging nowhere, he actually belongs everywhere and thereby gains an insight into historical change that is denied to ordinary mortals. Four *Gracchus* fragments survive, written by Kafka in April 1917 and published posthumously by Max Brod, who provided the title.

Kafka's oeuvre is peopled with inadequate incompetents, but it is a mistake to impose too rigid an autobiographical interpretation on all these characters. By January 1917, when he wrote *The Bridge* (Max Brod's title), Kafka had to a certain extent surmounted, for the time being, some of his domestic difficulties – his stories and anecdotes about father-son relationships had become less frequent, he seems to have controlled his feelings of guilt associated with his failure to marry Felice Bauer, he had moved into a house in the Alchimistengasse on the top of the castle hill, and he had started to embrace his mission as a writer with some confidence. Characters such as the protagonist in *The Bridge* who fails so comprehensibly to span the ravine are not so much self-portraits as self-caricatures. The same might also be said of the individual in *Give Up!*, an anecdote written during his last years, which Max Brod supplied with a title and published in 1936.

A Country Doctor, dedicated to Kafka's father, also dates from 1917, and was first published the following year. Like Gregor Samsa and many other characters in Kafka's work, the country doctor, in the story that bears the collection's title, is jolted out of his routine existence and confronted with human suffering: release from daily routine unleashes both spiritual and erotic energies. He becomes sexually aware of his maid Rosa and spiritually aware of the young man. While the priest remains at home 'picking his vestments apart', the doctor feels that it is his duty to heal the young man, but he considers himself too inadequate to do so and quite unable to save Rosa from the lecherous attentions of the stable-boy. In a diary entry of 15 September 1917 Kafka makes it clear that he regarded his own 'Lungenwunde' (tuberculosis) as the symbol of the spiritual wound that occurs so often in his works – a wound, he adds, that Felice Bauer had inflamed.

Outside the Law, though written in late 1914, was published as part of *A Country Doctor*, and was subsequently worked into the cathedral scene of *The Trial*, where it is told to K by the priest. The lowest doorkeeper represents those obstacles which man has to surmount if he is to win through to the spiritual authority that will give his life meaning. What makes the task more difficult is that these obstacles appear to have been manufactured by that same authority. The reader is therefore as perplexed as the man in the story and equally challenged to find a solution. In the novel, the priest and K discuss possible interpretations of the parable, and K becomes even more bewildered when the priest tells him that 'the correct understanding of a matter and misunderstanding the matter are not mutually exclusive' – a typical example of Kafka's use of paradox.

There are some thorny problems that face any translator of Kafka, none more so than the final word of *The Sentence*: 'In diesem Augenblick ging über die Brücke ein geradezu unendlicher Verkehr.' ('A quite endless stream of traffic was just crossing the bridge.') The basic meaning of the word 'Verkehr' is traffic, communication, and what Kafka partly implies is that Georg's lonely and isolated existence is at an end. One of a long line of bachelors who seem to be punished for living an unfulfilled and routine life, Georg suffered partly because of his self-imposed isolation. On his death there is a shift of narrative perspective – we no longer look at the world from Georg's viewpoint but from the narrator's. Georg is removed from the centre of the narrative, and the story ends with the description of bustling humanity crossing a crowded bridge. But 'Verkehr' also means 'sexual communication', 'sexual intercourse', and Kafka himself, commenting on the last line, confessed: 'Ich habe dabei an eine starke Ejakulation gedacht' ('I had in mind a violent ejaculation'). The problem for the translator is insuperable.

Equally taxing is the title of Kafka's most celebrated story, *Die Verwandlung*. In his letters to Felice Bauer – there is a detailed description of the genesis of the work in their correspondence – he also mentions the title without the definite article, 'Metamorphosis' instead of 'The Metamorphosis'. The concept of metamorphosis, however, is too slow for what actually happens to Gregor who is transformed overnight into a monstrous verminous insect. 'The Transformation', though it has little of the sensational ring of 'Metamorphosis', is arguably a more accurate translation. The word 'Ungeziefer' also raises problems. The opening sentence of Kafka's story reads: 'Als Gregor Samsa eines Morgens aus unruhigen Träumen erwachte, fand er sich zu einem ungeheuren Ungeziefer verwandelt' ('When Gregor Samsa woke one morning from uneasy dreams he found himself transformed in his bed into a monstrous insect.') The threefold use of the prefix 'un' is impossible to render into English, and the word 'Ungeziefer' has proved a stumbling-block ever since the publication of Willa and Edwin Muir's translation. The traditional rendering of 'Ungeziefer' as 'beetle' is misleading, since 'Ungeziefer' is a generic term, a collective noun meaning, quite simply, 'vermin'. Kafka never once reveals the kind of insect into which Gregor has been transformed, and though the cleaning woman calls Gregor 'an old dung-beetle' ('alter Mistkäfer') she is not attempting any entomological description but merely engaging in friendly banter. It should also be added that when Kurt Wolff, the publisher, submitted a sketch of the title-page which depicted Gregor as a beetle, Kafka was adamant that the insect could not be designed nor its shape disclosed. Though the OED lists several examples of 'vermin' used ungenerically and in the singular, it sounds odd nevertheless, and the best solution is probably to translate 'Ungeziefer' as 'insect'.

Too many translators of Kafka have intervened in matters of punctuation and paragraphing, abusing his idiosyncratic way with commas (which he often uses in preference to semi-colons), and creating shorter subdivisions from his larger and more unwieldy paragraphs. I have resisted such temptations, with the result that commas and long paragraphs proliferate when Kafka is at pains, as, for example, in *Give Up!* and *Outside the Law*, to reflect a character's psychological disorientation, or when he seeks to convey the frenzied pace of the action. I have also tried to do justice to Kafka's unorthodox sentence structure and precise use of language. It should be remembered that he spent five years studying law, and most of his professional life in the legal department of the Workers' Accident Insurance Office for the Kingdom of Bohemia, writing reports – available now in *Amtliche Schriften*, published by the East German Akademie Verlag in 1984 – in which clarity, detachment and accuracy were of paramount importance. A feature of his writing is the frequent use of antitheses through which he weighs up both sides of an argument with the result that even the most horrific nightmare is narrated with remarkable sobriety. More than almost any other German writer he employs adverbs such as 'allerdings' (admittedly), 'eigentlich' (actually), 'ein wenig' (a little), 'offenbar' (apparently), 'kaum' (hardly), 'ja' (after all), 'etwas' (somewhat), 'ganz' (wholly), 'wohl' (possibly) with almost pedantic care.

My translations have been made from the Kritische Ausgabe, edited by Jürgen Born, Gerhard Neumann, Malcolm Pasley and Jost Schillemeit, which corrected the many faulty readings of Kafka's handwriting that had blighted the earlier editions on which the first translations were based.

– Richard Stokes, 2002

Metamorphosis

I

When Gregor Samsa woke one morning from uneasy dreams he found himself transformed in his bed into a monstrous insect. He was lying on his hard shell-like back, and when he lifted his head a little he could see his dome-shaped brown body, banded with reinforcing arches, on top of which the blanket, ready to slip right off, maintained its precarious hold. His numerous legs, pitifully thin in relation to the rest of his bulk, danced ineffectually before his eyes.

'What has happened to me?' he thought. It was not a dream. His room, a normal though rather too small human room, lay peacefully between the four familiar walls. Above the table, on which a collection of cloth samples had been unpacked and laid out – Samsa was a travelling salesman – hung the picture that he had recently cut out of a magazine and mounted in a pretty gilt frame. It showed a lady in a fur hat and boa sitting up straight and holding out to the viewer a heavy fur muff into which her entire forearms had vanished.

Gregor's eyes then focused on the window, and the gloomy weather – you could hear raindrops beating on the metal window-sill – made him feel quite melancholy. 'Suppose I went back to sleep for a while and forgot all this nonsense,' he thought, but that was quite impossible, for he was used to sleeping on his right side and was unable in his present state to assume that position. No matter how vigorously he swung himself to the right, he kept rocking onto his back again. He must have tried it a hundred times, he shut his eyes to avoid looking at his flailing legs, and only gave up when he began to feel a faint dull ache in his side that he had never felt before.

'God,' he thought, 'what a strenuous profession I've chosen! On the road, day in, day out. Such business anxieties are much worse than those back home in the office, and in addition I'm lumbered with all this wretched travelling, the worry about train connections, the bad, irregular meals, the constantly changing, never lasting and never warm human relationships. To hell with it all!' He felt a slight itch up on his belly; pushed himself on his back slowly nearer to the bedpost in order to be able to lift his head better; located the itching spot, which was covered with a mass of tiny white dots he was unable to comprehend; and then tried to touch the spot with a leg, which he withdrew at once, however, since the contact sent an icy shiver through his body.

He slid back into his original position. 'These early mornings,' he thought, 'are very bad for the brain. A man needs his sleep. Other salesmen live like harem women. I mean, when I go back to the hotel during the morning to enter up the orders I've taken, those fellows are just sitting down to breakfast. If I tried that with my boss, I'd be sacked on the spot. Might not be a bad thing for me, after all. If it hadn't been for my parents, I'd have handed in my notice long ago, I'd have gone straight to my boss and given him a piece of my mind. He'd have fallen off his desk! Funny the way he sits on his desk and talks down to his staff from on high, especially as you have to come right up close because he's hard of hearing. Ah well, there's still a gleam of hope; once I've got the money together to pay back what my parents owe him – it might take another five or six years – I'll definitely do it. I'll make a fresh start. Meanwhile, though, I'd better get up, my train leaves at five.'

And he looked across to the alarm clock that was ticking on the chest of drawers. 'God almighty!' he thought. It was half past six and the hands were moving steadily forwards, in fact it was after half past, it was nearly a quarter to seven. Might the alarm not have rung? He could see from the bed that it had been set correctly to go off at four; it must have rung. Yes, but was it possible to sleep calmly through that furniture-shaking racket? Well, he hadn't exactly slept calmly, but that probably meant he had slept all the more soundly. But what should he do now? The next train left at seven; to catch that would mean a frantic rush, and the samples had not yet been packed, and he wasn't exactly feeling especially fresh and mobile. And even if he did catch the train, he could expect a thundering tirade from his boss, because the office boy would have met the five o'clock train and reported his absence long ago. The boy was his boss' lackey, a spineless, mindless creature. What if he were to report sick? But that would be highly embarrassing and suspicious, for during his five years with the firm Gregor had never once been sick. The boss would be bound to bring the health-insurance doctor round, reproach his parents for having an idle son, and cut short all their protests by quoting the doctor's view that the world consisted exclusively of perfectly healthy but work-shy people. And anyway, would he have been so wholly wrong in this instance? Apart from a certain drowsiness that was really quite superfluous after his long sleep, Gregor did feel well and even had an unusually hearty appetite.

While he was considering all this in the greatest haste, without being able to make up his mind to get out of bed – the alarm clock was just striking a quarter to seven – there was a cautious tap at the door near the top of his bed. 'Gregor,' called a voice – it was his mother – 'it's a quarter to seven. Didn't you have a train to catch?' That gentle voice! Gregor gave a start when he heard his own voice answer; it was unmistakably his own, but mingling with it, as if from below, was a painful, not-to-be-suppressed squeak that uttered the words clearly only for a second, before distorting them to such an extent that you wondered whether you had heard them properly. It had been Gregor's intention to answer at length and explain everything, but in the circumstances he confined himself to saying, 'Yes, yes, thank you mother, I'm just getting up.' Due to the wooden door the change in Gregor's voice was presumably not noticeable from outside, for his mother, reassured by this explanation, went shuffling off. But this brief exchange had alerted the other members of the family to the fact that Gregor, contrary to expectation, was still at home, and already his father was knocking at one of the side-doors, not hard, but with his fist. 'Gregor, Gregor,' he called, 'what is it?' And after a little while he repeated the reprimand in a deeper voice: 'Gregor! Gregor!' At the door on the other side, however, came the soft plaintive voice of his sister: 'Gregor? Aren't you well? Do you need anything?' 'Just coming,' Gregor replied in both directions and tried, through enunciating as clearly as possible and leaving long pauses between the words, to make his voice sound as inconspicuous as possible. His father went back to his breakfast, but his sister whispered, 'Gregor, open up, *please*.' But Gregor had no intention of opening the door, and congratulated himself instead on his prudent habit, adopted from his travels, of locking all the doors at night even when he was at home.

First of all he wanted to get up in peace and quiet, dress and above all have breakfast, and only then think about what to do next, for he knew that he would not reach any sensible conclusion as long as he was lying in bed. He recalled having fairly often felt some slight pain in bed, possibly as a result of lying awkwardly, which had turned out to be purely illusory once he was up, and he was curious to see how this morning's imaginings would gradually dissolve. There was not the slightest doubt in his mind that the change in his voice was simply the first symptom of a streaming cold, that occu-pational affliction of travelling salesmen.

Discarding the blanket was simple enough; he only needed to inflate himself a little, and it fell to the floor of its own accord. But after that things became more difficult because of his extraordinary girth. He would have needed arms and hands to lift himself up; instead he only had his numerous legs that were in constant and multifarious motion and over which he had no control. Whenever he tried to bend one, it straight-ened itself out, and by the time he finally managed to make this leg do his bidding, all the others were flailing around, as if liberated, in a state of most acute and painful excitement. 'Better not waste time in bed,' said Gregor to himself.

He tried at first to get the lower part of his body out of bed, but this lower part which he had incidentally not yet seen and of which he could form no really clear picture, proved too cumbersome; progress was so slow; and when at last, having become almost wild, he mustered all his strength and thrust himself recklessly forward, it turned out that he had chosen the wrong direction, he bumped violently against the bottom end of the bed, and the searing pain he felt informed him that it was precisely this lower part of his body that might for the time being be the most sensitive.

So he tried to get the upper part of his body out of bed first, twisting his head round to the edge of the bed. That was easy enough, and despite its girth and great weight, his body slowly followed the movement of his head. But when at long last he had got his head out over the side of the bed, in mid-air, he became afraid of continuing in this manner, for if he were to fall like that it would take a miracle for him not to sustain a head injury. And consciousness was the last thing he wanted to lose at the present time; he would rather stay in bed.

But when after a similar struggle he lay back panting in his original position, and saw again his little legs locked in what seemed to be even fiercer combat than before, and found no way of restoring any calm or order to such chaos, he told himself once more that there was no way he could stay in bed, and that the wisest thing would be to risk all for even the faintest hope of freeing himself from his bed. At the same time he did not forget to remind himself at intervals that the coolest of cool reflection was better by far than desperate decisions. At such moments he focused his eyes as sharply as possible on the window, but unfortunately the sight of the morning mist, which veiled even the other side of the narrow street, had little good cheer or encouragement to offer. 'Seven o'clock already,' he said to himself as the alarm clock rang once more, 'seven o'clock and still such a thick mist.' And for a short while he lay still, breathing quietly, hoping perhaps that such total silence might bring about a return to normal, everyday reality.

But then he said to himself: 'Before it strikes seven fifteen, I must at all costs be right out of bed. Anyway, someone by then will have come from the office to enquire about me, as the office opens before seven.' And he now set about rocking the whole length of his body evenly out of bed. If he let himself fall from the bed in this way, his head, which he intended to lift sharply as he fell, would presumably be unharmed. His back seemed to be hard; hitting the carpet would probably cause it no damage. His greatest concern was the thought of the loud noise he would inevitably make, and which would probably cause, if not alarm, then at least concern behind the various doors. But such a risk had to be taken.

When Gregor was already protruding halfway out of bed – the new method was not so much work as play, since he only needed to keep rocking in fits and starts – it occurred to him how simple everything would be if someone came to his aid. Two strong people – he had in mind his father and the maid – would be quite enough; they would only have to slide their arms under his arched back, slip him out of bed, bend their knees beneath the burden and then simply exercise patience till he somersaulted onto the floor, where the little legs would, he hoped, acquire a purpose. Well, quite apart from the fact that the doors were locked, ought he really to call for help? Despite his great predicament, he was unable to suppress a smile at the thought.

He had already reached the stage where, if he rocked fairly vigorously, he could scarcely keep his balance, and he would very soon have to make up his mind once and for all, because in five minutes it would be a quarter past seven – when there was a ring at the apartment door. 'Someone from the office,' he said to himself, and almost froze, while his little legs danced even faster. For a moment all was silent. 'They're not answering,' Gregor said to himself, seized by some insane hope. But then of course, as always, the maid strode purposefully to the door and opened it. Gregor only needed to hear the visitor's first word of greeting to know at once who it was – the chief clerk himself. Why was Gregor of all people condemned to work for a firm where the slightest lapse promptly aroused the greatest suspicion? Were all the employees scoundrels, then, every single one of them? Was there not a single loyal and devoted worker among them who, having failed to turn a mere two hours one morning to the firm's advantage, was driven so crazy with remorse that he was actually no longer capable of getting out of bed? Would it not have been sufficient to send an apprentice round to enquire – assuming that all these investigations were essential in the first place? Was it necessary for the chief clerk to come in person, necessary for the whole innocent family to be shown that the investigation of this suspicious affair could be entrusted to his wisdom alone? And more as a consequence of the agitation caused by these thoughts than as a result of true resolve, Gregor swung himself out of bed with all his might. There was a loud thump, but it was not a true bang. His fall had been muffled a little by the carpet, and his back was also more elastic than Gregor had supposed, hence the ensuing dull thud that was really not very conspicuous. He had not however been sufficiently careful with his head which he had banged, and which he twisted round and rubbed on the carpet in irritation and pain.

'Something's fallen in there,' said the chief clerk in the room on the left. Gregor tried to imagine whether something similar to what had just happened to him might one day happen to the chief clerk; he had to admit the possibility. But as if in brusque reply to this question, the chief clerk now took a few determined steps in the next room, causing his patent-leather boots to creak. From the room on the right Gregor's sister informed him in a whisper: 'Gregor, the chief clerk's here.' 'I know,' said Gregor to himself, but did not dare speak loud enough for his sister to hear.

'Gregor,' his father now said from the room on the left, 'the chief clerk has come to enquire why you didn't catch the early train. We don't know what to say to him. Besides, he'd like a word with you in person. So please open up. He'll be kind enough, I'm sure, to excuse the mess in your room.' 'Good morning, Herr Samsa,' came meanwhile the friendly voice of the chief clerk. 'He's not well,' Gregor's mother told the chief clerk, while his father was still talking outside the door, 'he's not well, sir, believe you me. Why else would Gregor miss a train! That boy thinks of nothing but his work. It almost makes me angry that he never goes out in the evening; he's been in town all week but stayed at home every evening. He sits with us at table and quietly reads the newspaper or pores over timetables. Fretwork provides his only amusement. He made a little picture-frame, for example, which took him two or three evenings; you'll be amazed how pretty it is; it's hanging in his room; you'll see it in a moment when Gregor opens the door. I'm glad, by the way, that you have come, sir; we'd never have persuaded Gregor to unlock the door by ourselves; he's so stubborn, and he's certainly unwell, although he denied it this morning.' 'Just coming,' Gregor said slowly and deliberately, and kept quite still so as not to miss a word of the conversation. 'I too, madam, can think of no other explanation,' said the chief clerk. 'I hope it's nothing serious. Although I have to say that we businessmen are – unfortunately or fortunately, as you will – very often obliged for business reasons simply to shrug off minor indispositions.' 'Can the chief clerk come in now?' his father asked impatiently, knocking on the door again. 'No,' said Gregor. In the room on the left an embarrassed silence fell; in the room on the right his sister began to sob.

Why did his sister not join the others? She had probably only just got out of bed and hadn't even begun to dress. And why was she crying? Because he was not getting up to let the chief clerk in, because he was in danger of losing his job, and because the boss would then start hounding his parents again about those old debts? There was surely no need to worry about such things for the time being. Gregor was still present and had not the slightest intention of deserting his family. For the moment, it was true, he was lying there on the carpet, and no one aware of his condition could seriously have expected him to let the chief clerk in. But this minor discourtesy, for which a suitable excuse could easily be found at a later stage, was surely not reason enough to dismiss Gregor on the spot. And it seemed to Gregor that it would have been much more sensible to leave him alone, instead of disturbing him with tears and entreaties. But it was, of course, the uncertainty which was distressing the others, and that excused their behaviour.

'Herr Samsa,' the chief clerk now called out in a louder voice, 'what is wrong? You barricade yourself in your room, answer nothing but yes or no, cause your parents a great deal of unnecessary anxiety and, in addition – I only mention this in passing – neglect your professional duties in a frankly quite outrageous manner. On behalf of your parents and your employer I must ask you most earnestly for an immediate, an unambiguous explanation. I am astonished, astonished. I had always considered you to be a calm and reasonable individual, and now you suddenly seem inclined to flaunt these peculiar whims. Although your superior intimated to me this morning a possible explanation for your absence – concerning the cash payments that you had been trusted to collect – I virtually gave him my word of honour that there could be no truth in such an explanation. But faced here with your incomprehensible obstinacy, I find myself losing absolutely all inclination to defend you in any way whatsoever. And your position is far from secure. My original intention was to tell you all this privately, but as you are causing me to waste my time here so aimlessly, I see no reason why your good parents should not hear it as well. So: your achievements have recently been most unsatisfactory; it is of course not the best season for doing business, we recognise that; but there is no such thing, Herr Samsa, there can be no such thing as a season for doing no business at all.'

'But sir,' cried Gregor, distraught and forgetting everything else in his agitation, 'I'll open the door immediately, at once. A slight indisposition, a bout of dizziness, prevented me from getting up. I'm still in bed. But now I feel perfectly fit again. I'm just getting out of bed. Just be patient for a second! Things aren't as good as I thought. But there's nothing wrong with me. It's strange how quickly something like that can hit you! I was feeling fine only last night, you can ask my parents, or, wait, I did have a feeling last night that something was wrong. It must have shown on my face. Why on earth didn't I let the office know? But one always imagines one will shake off such things without needing to stay at home. Sir! Spare my parents! All these accusations of yours are quite unfounded; and no one has said a word about them to me. Perhaps you haven't seen the last batch of orders I sent in. Anyway, I'll catch the eight o'clock train, the few hours' rest have done me good. Don't waste another moment, sir; I'll be at the office myself in no time, would you kindly pass that on and send my respects to the boss!'

And while Gregor was blurting all this out and hardly knew what he was saying, he had managed to reach the chest of drawers without difficulty, as a consequence perhaps of the practice he had acquired in bed, and was now trying to haul himself upright. He really did intend to open the door, really did intend to show himself and speak with the chief clerk; he was anxious to find out what the others, who were asking for him with such insistence, would say when they saw him. If they took fright, Gregor would have no further responsibility and could relax. If, on the other hand, they took it all in their stride, there would be no reason for him to get agitated, and he could, if he hurried, actually be at the station by eight. At first he kept sliding down the smooth surface of the chest of drawers, but at last he gave himself a final heave and stood upright; he no longer paid any attention to the pains in his nether regions, no matter how acute they were. He now let himself slump against the back of a nearby chair, gripping it round the edge with his little legs. Having thus gained control over himself, he fell silent, for he was now able to listen to what the chief clerk was saying.

'Have you understood a single word?' the chief clerk was asking his parents, 'he isn't trying to make fools of us, is he?' 'God forbid,' cried his mother, already in tears, 'perhaps he's seriously ill, and we're tormenting him. Grete! Grete!' she then cried. 'Mother?' called his sister from the other side. They were communicating through Gregor's room. 'You must go to the doctor's at once. Gregor is ill. Fetch the doctor, quick. Did you hear Gregor talking just now?' 'That was the voice of an animal,' said the chief clerk, in a tone that was strikingly soft compared to his mother's shrieking. 'Anna! Anna!' his father was shouting through the hallway into the kitchen, and he clapped his hands. 'Get a locksmith immediately!' And already the two girls were running with rustling skirts through the hall – how had his sister got dressed so quickly? – and tearing open the apartment door. There was no sound of the door slamming; they had probably left it open, as happens in homes where a great calamity has occurred.

But Gregor had become much calmer. It was true, then, that they could no longer understand his words, though they had seemed clear enough to him, clearer than before, perhaps because his ear had become attuned to them. But at least they now believed that all was not quite right with him, and were prepared to help. The confidence and assurance with which the first steps had been taken comforted him. He felt integrated once more into human society and hoped for great and startling contributions from both the doctor and the locksmith, without really making any clear distinction between them. In order to make his voice as clear as possible for the crucial discussions that were imminent, he gave a little cough, taking good care, of course, to muffle it properly, since possibly even that noise might sound different from human coughing, something that he no longer felt competent to judge. Complete silence had meanwhile fallen in the adjoining room. Perhaps his parents were sitting at the table with the chief clerk, whispering; perhaps they were all leaning against the wall, listening.

Gregor slowly dragged himself towards the door, pushing the chair in front of him, then let go of it, threw himself against the door, where he propped himself up – the pads on the bottom of his little legs were slightly adhesive – and rested there for a moment from his exertions. But then he set about turning the key in the lock with his mouth. Unfortunately it seemed that he had no proper teeth – what was he to grasp the key with? – but to compensate for that his jaws were very strong; with their help he actually got the key moving, ignoring the fact that in so doing he was undoubtedly causing himself some damage, for a brown liquid issued from his mouth, flowed over the key and dripped onto the floor. 'Listen,' said the chief clerk in the next room, 'he's turning the key.' That was a great encouragement to Gregor; but they should all have been cheering him on, his father and mother too. 'Come on, Gregor,' they should have shouted, 'stick at it, harder, work on that lock!' And imagining that they were all following his efforts with tense excitement, he bit furiously on the key with all the strength he could muster. As the key turned, he danced round the lock; he was now holding himself up by his mouth alone and, as the situation demanded, either clung to the key or pressed it down again with the full weight of his body. The sharper sound of the lock as it finally snapped back woke Gregor up once and for all. With a sigh of relief he said to himself, 'I didn't need the locksmith after all,' and laid his head on the handle to pull the door wide open.

By opening it in this way, the door was actually wide open while he himself was still not visible. First he had to edge his way round this wing of the door, and with the utmost care, if he wasn't to fall flat on his back before entering the room. He was still preoccupied with this tricky manoeuvre, and had no time to attend to anything else, when he heard the chief clerk utter a loud 'Ugh!' – it sounded like a rush of wind – and now he could see him, standing closest to the door, pressing his hand to his open mouth, backing slowly away, as if driven out by some invisible and constantly unrelenting force. His mother – in spite of the chief clerk's presence, she was standing there with her hair all undone and tousled from the night – looked first with clasped hands at his father, then took two steps towards Gregor and slumped down, her skirts billowing in circles around her, her face completely buried in her bosom. His father looked hostile and clenched a fist, as if he intended to beat Gregor back into his room, then looked uncertainly round the living-room, shaded his eyes with his hands and wept until his powerful chest shook.

Gregor did not in fact enter the room at all, but leaned against the inside of the firmly bolted wing of the door, so all that could be seen was half of his body and, above it, his head tilted to one side and staring out at the others. In the meantime it had grown much lighter; clearly visible on the other side of the street was a section of the endless, grey-black building opposite – it was a hospital – with its regular windows harshly piercing its façade; the rain was still falling, but only in huge, individually visible drops that were literally pelting the ground one by one. An excessive number of breakfast dishes lay scattered on the table, since breakfast for his father was the most important meal of the day, which he would prolong for hours by reading a variety of newspapers. Hanging on the wall opposite was a photograph of Gregor from his army days, which showed him as a lieutenant, hand on sword, a carefree smile on his lips, inviting respect for his bearing and uniform. The door to the hallway was open, and since the front door was open too, it was possible to see out onto the landing and the top of the stairs.

'Right,' said Gregor, well aware that he was the only one to have retained his composure, 'I shall now get dressed, pack my samples and be off. Are you willing, are you willing to let me go? You can see, sir, that I am not stubborn and that I like my work; travelling is wearisome, but I couldn't live without it. Where are you going, sir? To the office? Yes? Will you make a faithful report of all this? A man might for a moment be unable to work, but that's precisely the time to remember his past achievements and to consider that later on, once the obstacle has been removed, he will be sure to work with increased energy and concentration. I am deeply beholden to the head of the firm, as you are well aware. On the other hand, I have my parents and my sister to think about. I'm in a tight spot, but I'll work my way out of it. Don't make things harder for me than they already are. Speak up for me in the firm! Travelling salesmen aren't well-liked, I know. People think they earn a fortune and live in clover. They have no particular reason to revise such a prejudice. But you, sir, you have a better view of things than the rest of the staff and, between you and me, than the head of the firm himself who, in his capacity as employer, can easily allow his judgement to err, to the disadvantage of an employee. And you know very well that the travelling salesman, who is out of the office practically all year round, can fall prey to gossip, coincidences and unfounded complaints, against which he's completely unable to defend himself, since in most cases he knows nothing at all about them, or only finds out for himself when he has just returned exhausted from a trip and hears of the repercussions at home, when it's too late to discover their cause. Sir, don't go away without telling me that you think I'm at least partly right!'

But the chief clerk had already turned away at Gregor's very first words, merely staring back at him with curled lips over his quivering shoulder. And during Gregor's speech he never stood still for a moment but, without letting Gregor out of his sight, kept moving away towards the door, only very gradually though, as if there were some secret injunction against leaving the room. He was already in the hallway, and to judge from the sudden movement with which he finally stepped from the living-room, one might have thought he had just scorched the sole of his foot. Once in the hall, however, he stretched out his right hand far in front of him towards the stairs, as if an almost supernatural deliverance were awaiting him there.

Gregor realised that he could in no circumstances allow the chief clerk to depart in this frame of mind if his position in the firm were not to be seriously endangered. His parents did not understand these things too well; in the course of many years they had formed the conviction that Gregor was set up for life in this firm; and besides, they were so preoccupied with their own immediate worries that they had completely lost the ability to look ahead. But Gregor had this ability. The chief clerk must be restrained, calmed down, convinced and finally won over; Gregor's future and that of his family depended on it! If only his sister had been there! She was clever; she had already started to cry when Gregor was still lying calmly on his back. And surely the chief clerk, this ladies' man, would have allowed himself to be swayed by her; she would have closed the front door and talked him out of his fears in the hall. But since his sister was not there, Gregor had to act on his own. And without stopping to think that he was still wholly unfamiliar with his present powers of locomotion, without stopping to think that his words had possibly, even probably, not been understood again, he let go of the wing of the door; he shoved himself through the opening; he wanted to get to the chief clerk who was by now, ridiculously, holding onto the banisters with both hands; but promptly fell, as he groped for support, onto his numerous little legs with a short cry. No sooner had this happened than, for the first time that morning, he felt a sense of physical well-being; his little legs had firm ground beneath them; they obeyed him completely, as he noted to his joy; they were even eager to carry him wherever he wanted to go; and he already believed that an end to all his suffering was finally at hand. But at that very same moment, as he lay there on the ground rocking to and fro with repressed motion, not far from his mother and directly opposite her, she, who had seemed so utterly self-absorbed, suddenly leapt into the air, arms stretched out wide, fingers spread, crying, 'Help, for God's sake, help!', craned her neck forward as if to see Gregor better, but in self-contradiction ran frantically back instead; forgot that the table with the breakfast things was behind her; sat down on it hastily, absent-mindedly, when she reached it; and seemed quite unaware that the coffee was pouring onto the carpet in a steady stream out of the big overturned pot.

'Mother, mother,' said Gregor softly, and looked up at her. For a moment he had completely forgotten about the chief clerk, though at the sight of the coffee pouring out he couldn't resist snapping at the air several times with his jaws. At this his mother let out another scream, fled from the table and fell into the arms of his father who came rushing up to her. But Gregor now had no time for his parents; the chief clerk was already on the stairs; his chin on the banister, he was taking a last look back. Gregor darted forwards to be as sure as possible of catching up with him; the chief clerk must have suspected something, for he leapt down several steps and disappeared; he was still yelling 'Ugh!', and it echoed through the whole staircase. Unfortunately, his father, who till then had remained relatively composed, seemed quite bewildered by the chief clerk's flight, for instead of running after the chief clerk himself or at least not obstructing Gregor in his pursuit, he seized in his right hand the chief clerk's cane, which had been left behind on a chair with his hat and overcoat, picked up with his left hand a large newspaper from the table and, stamping his feet and brandishing both cane and newspaper, began to drive Gregor back into his room. Gregor's entreaties were to no avail, none were even understood; however humbly he turned his head, his father only stamped his feet harder. On the other side of the room his mother had thrown open a window despite the cool weather, and, leaning a long way out, was pressing her face into her hands. A strong draught was created between the street and the stairwell, the curtains billowed, the newspapers on the table rustled, several sheets blew across the floor. Relentlessly his father drove him back, hissing like a savage. Gregor, however, still had no practice in walking backwards, and was making very slow progress. If only Gregor had been allowed to turn round, he could have reached his room in no time at all, but he was frightened of making his father impatient by so time-consuming a turn, and at any moment the cane in his father's hand threatened to deal him a deadly blow on the back or the head. Finally, however, Gregor had no alternative, for he noticed with horror that in reverse he could not even keep going in one direction; so he now began, with repeated and anguished sideways glances at his father, to turn around as quickly as he could, which was in reality very slowly. Perhaps his father was aware of his good intentions, because he did not hinder him in this, but occasionally, from a distance, even directed the operation with the tip of his stick. If only his father had not kept making those intolerable hissing noises! It threw Gregor into utter confusion. He had almost turned himself completely round when, with his mind continually on this hissing, he made an error and started turning the other way. But when he had finally succeeded in facing the doorway, it became clear that his body was too broad to pass through as it was. His father, of course, in his present state of mind, did not even consider opening the other wing of the door in order to give Gregor sufficient room to pass through. He was obsessed by the one idea of getting Gregor back to his room as quickly as possible. He would never have countenanced the elaborate pre-parations that would have been necessary for Gregor to assume an upright position and perhaps in that way pass through the door. Instead he drove Gregor on, as if there were no obstacle, with exceptional loudness; it no longer sounded like the voice of a single father behind Gregor; it was now beyond a joke, and Gregor thrust himself – come what may – into the doorway. One side of his body rose up, he lay lopsided in the doorway, one of his flanks was rubbed quite raw, the white door was stained with ugly blotches, soon he would be stuck fast unable to move unaided, his little legs on one side hung quivering in the air, those on the other were squashed painfully against the floor – at which point his father dealt him a truly liberating blow from behind, and, bleeding profusely, he flew far into his room. The door was then slammed shut with the cane, and at last there was silence.

II

It was not until dusk that Gregor woke from his deep, coma-like sleep. He would certainly have woken not much later even without being disturbed, for he felt sufficiently rested and refreshed, but it seemed to him that he had been roused by hurried steps and a cautious closing of the door that led into the hall. The light of the electric street lamps flickered pallidly on the ceiling and the upper parts of the furniture, but down where Gregor lay it was dark. Slowly, still groping awkwardly with his feelers, which he was only now beginning to appreciate, he dragged himself over to the door to see what had been happening there. His left side felt like one long, unpleasantly tautening scar, and he was reduced to limping on his twin rows of legs. One leg, moreover, had been seriously damaged in the course of the morning's events – it was almost a miracle that only one had been damaged – and trailed limply after him.

Only when he reached the door did he notice what had actually lured him there; it was the smell of something to eat. For there stood a bowl brimming with sweetened milk in which little slices of white bread were floating. He could almost have laughed for joy, because he was even hungrier than he had been in the morning, and he promptly dipped his head into the milk, almost up to his eyes. But he soon drew it back again in disappointment; not merely because eating caused him difficulties due to his tender left side – and he could only eat if his whole panting body participated – but because he did not care for the milk at all, despite it normally being his favourite drink, for which reason his sister had certainly put it down for him. Indeed he turned away from the bowl with repugnance and crawled back into the middle of the room.

In the living-room the gas had already been lit, as Gregor could see through the crack in the door, but whereas at this time of day his father always used to read aloud extracts from his evening paper to his mother and sometimes his sister as well, everything now was utterly silent. Maybe this custom of reading aloud, which his sister was always telling him about and mentioning in letters, had recently been discontinued. But it was just as silent in all the rooms, even though the apartment was surely not empty. 'What a quiet life the family has been leading,' Gregor said to himself, and felt so proud, as he sat there staring into the darkness, that he had been able to provide his parents and sister with a life of this sort in such a pleasant apartment. But what if all the peace, the prosperity, the contentment were now to come to a terrible end? In order not to lose himself in such thoughts, Gregor chose to move about, and crawled back and forth across the room.

During the long evening, first one of the side-doors and then the other was opened slightly and quickly shut again; somebody had presumably needed to come in, but had had too many misgivings. Gregor now stationed himself directly in front of the living-room door, determined somehow to get his hesitant visitor into the room, or at least to discover who it might be; but the door was not opened again and Gregor waited in vain. In the morning, when the doors had been locked, everyone had wanted to come in; now, when he had opened one door and the others had clearly been opened during the day, no one came any more, and the keys, moreover, were now on the outside.

It wasn't until late in the evening that the light was turned off in the living-room, and it quickly became clear that his parents and his sister had stayed up all that time, for all three of them could now be distinctly heard moving away on tiptoe. Certainly no one would now come into Gregor's room until morning; he therefore had a long time to consider in peace and quiet how best to reorganise his life. But the high-ceilinged spacious room, in which he was obliged to lie flat on the floor, filled him with an anguish he could not account for, since it was, after all, the room he had lived in for the past five years – and with a half-conscious change of direction and not without a slight feeling of shame he scuttled under the couch where, although his back was a little squashed and he could not raise his head any more, he immediately felt quite comfortable and was only sorry that his body was too broad to fit completely beneath the couch.

There he stayed the whole night, either dozing and being continually jolted awake by pangs of hunger, or in worries and vague hopes, all of which, however, led to the conclusion that for the time being he had to stay calm and, by exercising patience and being as considerate as possible to his family, make bearable the unpleasantnesses that he was compelled to cause them in his present condition.

By early next morning – it was still almost night – Gregor had an opportunity to test the firmness of his new resolve, for his sister, almost fully dressed, opened the door from the hall and looked uneasily in. She did not see him immediately, but when she spotted him beneath the couch – good heavens, he had to be somewhere, he couldn't just have flown away – she got such a fright that she lost control of herself and slammed the door shut again from the outside. But, as if regretting her behaviour, she immediately opened the door again and tiptoed into the room, as though she were visiting someone seriously ill, or even a stranger. Gregor had stuck his head out almost to the edge of the couch, and was observing her. Would she notice that he had left the milk standing, though not because he had no appetite, far from it, and would she bring in some other food that suited him better? If she didn't do so of her own accord, he would rather starve than bring it to her attention, although in fact he felt a tremendous urge to dart out from under the couch, throw himself at his sister's feet and beg her to bring him something good to eat. His sister, however, noticed immediately, and with astonishment, the still-full bowl, from which only a little milk had splattered all around, picked it up, admittedly not with her bare hands but with a cloth, and carried it out. Gregor was extremely curious to know what she would bring instead, and indulged in all manner of speculation. But never could he have guessed what his sister in the goodness of her heart actually did. In order to find out what he liked, she brought him a whole selection of things, all spread out on an old newspaper: old, half-rotten vegetables; bones left over from supper, surrounded by congealed white sauce; some raisins and almonds; some cheese that two days earlier Gregor had declared inedible; a slice of dry bread, a slice of bread and butter, and another spread with butter and salted. In addition to all this she also put down the bowl, which had probably been permanently assigned to Gregor, and into which she had poured some water. And out of a sense of delicacy, since she knew that Gregor would not eat in her presence, she hastily withdrew and even turned the key in the lock to let Gregor know that he could make himself as comfortable as he wished. Gregor's little legs whirred as he made his way to the food. His wounds, moreover, must have completely healed by now, for he felt no further impediment, which astonished him, and he remembered how more than a month earlier he had cut his finger ever so slightly with a knife and how this finger had still been hurting him only the day before yesterday. 'Might I have grown less sensitive?' he thought, already sucking greedily on the cheese which had attracted him immediately and more forcibly than all the other food. In quick succession and with tears of contentment welling in his eyes, he devoured the cheese, the vegetables and the sauce; the fresh food, on the other hand, did not appeal to him, he couldn't even stand the smell and he actually dragged the things he did not wish to eat a little further off. He had long finished everything and was just lying lazily on the same spot when, as a sign that he should withdraw, his sister slowly turned the key. That immediately made him start, despite the fact that he was almost dozing off, and he scuttled back beneath the couch. But it took enormous self-control to stay under the couch, even for the short time that his sister was in the room, since the copious meal had bloated his body a little and he could hardly breathe in that cramped space. In between brief bouts of suffocation he watched with slightly bulging eyes as his unsuspecting sister took a broom and swept up not only the remains of what he had eaten but even the food that Gregor had not touched, as if it too were now unusable, and then dumped everything hastily into a bucket which she covered with a wooden lid, before carrying everything out. She had hardly turned her back when Gregor came out from under the couch to stretch and distend his belly.

This was how Gregor now received his food each day, once in the morning while his parents and the maid were still asleep, and again when everyone had had lunch, for then his parents took another short nap and the maid was sent on some errand or other by his sister. They surely did not want him to starve either, but perhaps the only way they could bear to find out about his eating habits was by hearsay, perhaps his sister even wanted to spare them what was possibly merely a minor distress, for they were really suffering enough as it was.

What pretexts had been used on that first morning to get the doctor and the locksmith out of the apartment, Gregor was quite unable to discover, for since the others could not understand what he said, it did not occur to anyone, not even his sister, that he might be able to understand other people, and so when his sister was in his room he had to content himself with hearing her intermittent sighs and invocations to the saints. It was only later, when she had begun to get used to everything – there could never of course be any question of a complete adjustment – that Gregor sometimes seized on a remark that was meant to be friendly or could be so interpreted. 'He really liked his food today,' she would say when Gregor had licked his bowl clean, and when the opposite was true, which gradually occurred more and more frequently, she would say almost sadly: 'He's left everything again.'

But although Gregor could not discover anything directly, he did overhear a fair amount from the adjoining rooms, and whenever he heard voices he would run at once to the appropriate door and press his whole body against it. Especially in the early days there was no conversation that did not in some way, if only clandestinely, refer to him. For two whole days there were consultations to be heard at every meal about how they should now proceed; but the same topic was also discussed between meals, for at least two members of the family were always at home, probably because no one wanted to be at home alone and because leaving the apartment completely empty was out of the question. Besides, the maid had on the very first day – it was not quite clear what or how much she knew of what had happened – gone to his mother and begged her on bended knees to be dismissed at once, and when she took her leave a quarter of an hour later, she thanked them in tears for her dismissal, as if it had been the greatest favour ever conferred on her, and vowed, without any prompting, a fearful oath that she would never breathe a word to anyone.

Now Gregor's sister, with her mother's help, had to do the cooking as well; although that did not of course involve much work since they ate practically nothing. Time and again Gregor heard one of them vainly exhorting the other to eat, and never getting any other answer than, 'Thank you, I've had enough,' or something similar. They didn't seem to drink anything either. His sister often asked his father if he wanted a beer, and kindly offered to fetch it herself, and when his father made no reply she said, in order to remove any misgivings he might have, that she could send the janitor's wife to fetch it, whereupon his father uttered a decisive 'No', and that was the last they heard of it.

In the course of the very first day his father explained fully the family's financial situation and prospects to both mother and sister. From time to time he rose from the table and took some receipt or notebook out of his small Wertheim safe that he had held onto even after the collapse of his business five years earlier. He could be heard opening the complicated lock and closing it again once he had taken out what he was looking for. These explanations by his father were to some extent the first encouraging news he had heard since his imprisonment.

He had always assumed that his father had been left with nothing at all from that business, at least his father had never told him anything to the contrary, and Gregor himself had never asked him. Gregor's sole concern in those days had been to do everything in his power to help his family forget as quickly as possible the commercial disaster that had plunged them all into utter despair. And so he had set to work with quite exceptional zeal and risen almost overnight from junior clerk to travelling salesman, in which capacity he naturally had many more possibilities of earning money, since his successes could be immediately translated by way of commission into ready cash that could be laid on the table at home before the astonished and delighted eyes of his family. Those had been wonderful times, which had never been repeated, at least not so gloriously, although Gregor subsequently earned so much money that he was in a position to meet the entire family's expenses and actually did so. They had simply got used to it, the family as well as Gregor; they accepted the money with gratitude, he gave it with pleasure, but no special feelings of warmth were engendered any more. Only his sister had remained close to Gregor, and it had been his secret plan that she, who, unlike him, loved music and could play the violin most movingly, should be sent next year to the conservatoire, regardless of the great expense it would entail and which he would somehow meet. During Gregor's short stays in town, the conservatoire would often crop up in conversations with his sister, but never as anything more than a beautiful dream which could not possibly be fulfilled, and their parents did not even like to hear these innocent allusions; Gregor, however, had very fixed ideas on the subject, and intended to make the solemn announcement on Christmas Eve.

Such were the thoughts, utterly futile in his present

condition, that passed through his mind as he clung there upright, glued to the door, and listened. Sometimes out of general exhaustion he could not pay attention any longer and let his head bump carelessly against the door, but he immediately held it up again, for even the tiny noise this made had been heard in the next room and reduced them all to silence. 'What on earth is he up to now,' said his father after a while, obviously turning towards the door, and only then would the interrupted conversation gradually be resumed.

Gregor now became thoroughly acquainted – for his father was in the habit of repeating himself frequently in his explanations, partly because he had not concerned himself with these matters for quite some time and partly because his mother could not always grasp things on first hearing – with the fact that, despite all their misfortune, a sum of money, admittedly very small, was still intact from the old days, which in the interim had increased a little with the untouched interest. But besides that, the money Gregor had brought home every month – he had kept only a few gulden for himself – had not all been used up and had accumulated into a modest capital. Gregor nodded vigorously behind his door, delighted at this unexpected foresight and thrift. He could in fact have used this surplus money to pay off more of his father's debts to his boss, thus bringing much closer the day when he could quit his job, but as things stood, the way his father had arranged it was undoubtedly better.

Yet this money was by no means sufficient for the family even to consider living off the interest; it might have sufficed to support them for one, or at most two years, but that was all. It was therefore merely a sum that should not actually be touched but rather put aside for an emergency; money to live on had to be earned. Now Gregor's father, though in good health, was an old man who had not worked for five years, and could not in any case be expected to take on too much; during those five years, the first holiday of his arduous yet unsuccessful life, he had put on a lot of fat and had consequently become very sluggish. And was Gregor's old mother now supposed to go out and earn money when, suffering as she did from asthma, she found it a strain even to walk round the flat and spent every other day lying on the sofa by the open window gasping for breath? And was his sister now to go out to work, who at seventeen was still a child and whose way of life no one would have begrudged her, consisting as it did of dressing prettily, sleeping late, helping in the house, enjoying a few modest amusements and above all playing the violin? Whenever the conversation turned to this need to earn money, Gregor would first let go of the door and then throw himself down on the cool leather sofa beside it, for he felt quite hot with shame and grief.

Often he would lie there all night long, not sleeping a wink but merely scratching at the leather for hours on end. Or, not shirking the huge effort of pushing a chair to the window, he would crawl up to the window-sill and, propped up in the chair, lean against the window, evidently responding to a vague memory of that sense of freedom which looking out of the window had once given him. For as the days went by he did in fact see things even a short distance away less and less distinctly; the hospital opposite, which he used to curse because he saw so much of it, he could now no longer see at all, and had he not known perfectly well that he lived in the quiet but decidedly urban Charlottenstrasse, he might have thought that what he saw from his window was a wilderness in which the grey sky and grey earth were indistinguishably mingled. His thoughtful sister only needed to see the chair by the window on two occasions before she thereafter, each time she had finished tidying his room, pushed it carefully back beneath the window and even, from then on, left the inner casement open.

If only Gregor had been able to speak to his sister and thank her for everything that she had to do for him, he could have accepted her efforts more easily; but as it was, they caused him pain. His sister certainly tried to ease the embarrassment of the whole situation as much as she could, and as time went on she became more and more successful, but with time Gregor too saw everything much more clearly. Her very entrance was terrible for him. The moment she crossed the threshold, without pausing to shut the door, even though she was other-wise most careful to spare everyone the sight of Gregor's room, she ran straight to the window, hastily tore it open, as if she were almost suffocating, remained there a while, no matter how cold it was, breathing deeply. She terrified Gregor twice daily with all this crashing around; he spent the whole time trembling beneath the couch, even though he knew perfectly well that she would certainly have spared him this, if only she had been capable of staying in a room occupied by Gregor with the window closed.

Once, it must have been a month since Gregor's trans-formation, and there was no particular reason now for his sister to be astonished at his appearance, she came a little earlier than usual and caught Gregor, motionless and at his most terrifying, looking out of the window. It would not have surprised Gregor if she had not come in, because his position prevented her from opening the window at once, but not only did she not come in, she even sprang back and shut the door; a stranger might almost have thought that Gregor had been lying in wait for her, intending to bite her. Gregor of course immediately hid himself beneath the couch, but he had to wait until noon before his sister returned, and she seemed much more restless than usual. He realised from this that the sight of him was still unbearable to her and was bound to remain unbearable, and that it probably required enormous self-control on her part not to run away at the sight of even the small portion of his body that jutted out from under the couch. And in order to spare her this sight, he managed one day – the task took him four hours – to carry the bedsheet on his back over to the couch and drape it in such a way that he was now completely covered, making it impossible for his sister to see him, even if she bent down. Had she considered this sheet unnecessary, she could of course have removed it, for it was clear enough that it gave Gregor no pleasure to close himself off so completely, but she left the sheet the way it was, and Gregor even thought he detected a look of gratitude when, in order to see how his sister was taking the new arrangement, he cautiously raised the sheet a little with his head.

For the first fortnight his parents could not bring themselves to enter his room, and he often heard them wholeheartedly acknowledging the work his sister was now doing, whereas before they had frequently been annoyed with her because she seemed to them a somewhat unhelpful girl. But now both of them, his father and his mother, often waited outside Gregor's room, while his sister cleaned it out, and as soon as she emerged, she had to give them a detailed account of how the room looked, what Gregor had eaten, how he had behaved this time, and whether he had perhaps shown a slight improvement. His mother, incidentally, wanted to visit Gregor relatively early on, but his father and sister succeeded at first in dissuading her with rational arguments, to which Gregor listened most attentively and with unreserved approval. Later, though, she had to be restrained by force, and when she cried out: 'Let me see my Gregor, my own unhappy son! Don't you understand that I must go to him?', Gregor thought it might be a good thing after all if his mother came in, not every day of course, but perhaps once a week; she really did understand everything so much better than his sister who, for all her courage, was still only a child and had perhaps, when all was said and done, only taken on so hard a task out of childish recklessness.

Gregor's wish to see his mother was soon fulfilled. During the day Gregor did not want to show himself at the window, if only out of consideration for his parents, but neither could he crawl very much on the few square yards of floor, even at night he found it difficult to lie still, eating soon stopped giving him the slightest pleasure, and so for amusement he acquired the habit of crawling all over the walls and ceiling. He was particularly partial to hanging from the ceiling; it was quite different from lying on the floor; one could breathe more freely; a mild vibration coursed through his body; and in the almost happy absent-mindedness which Gregor experienced up there, it sometimes happened that to his own surprise he let go and crashed to the floor. But now of course he had his body under much better control than before and even such a great fall did him no harm. His sister noticed at once the new pastime that Gregor had discovered for himself – after all, he left behind traces of his sticky substance even when crawling – and decided to give Gregor as much crawling-space as possible by removing the furniture which stood in his way, especially the chest of drawers and the desk. But she was unable to do this on her own; she dared not ask her father to help; the maid would most certainly not have helped, for although this girl of about sixteen had been braving it out since the dismissal of the previous cook, she had asked as a favour to be allowed to keep the kitchen locked at all times and open it only when specifically called on to do so; so his sister had no alternative but to fetch his mother when her father was out. And his mother did come, uttering cries of excitement and joy, though she fell silent at the door of Gregor's room. First, of course, his sister checked whether all was well within; only then did she let her mother enter. Gregor had very hastily pulled the sheet down even lower, creating more folds – the whole thing really did look like a sheet that had been randomly thrown over the couch. Once again Gregor refrained from peering out from under the sheet; on this occasion he denied himself the sight of his mother and was simply happy that she had come. 'Come on, you can't see him,' said his sister, evidently leading his mother by the hand. Gregor could now hear the two frail women shifting the old heavy chest of drawers from its place, with his sister continually bearing the main burden and ignoring the anxious warnings of his mother, who was afraid she might overtax herself. It took a very long time. After they had been at it for what must have been a good quarter of an hour, his mother said it would be better to leave the chest of drawers where it was, for in the first place it was simply too heavy and they would not finish before his father arrived, and with the chest in the middle of the room they would be blocking Gregor's every move, and secondly it was by no means certain that by removing the furniture they were doing Gregor a favour. It seemed to her that the opposite was the case; she found the sight of the bare wall downright depressing; and why shouldn't Gregor share the same feeling, since he had long before grown used to these pieces of furniture and would therefore feel abandoned in the empty room. 'And wouldn't it look,' his mother concluded very quietly, in fact she had been almost whispering the whole time, as if she wanted to prevent Gregor, whose precise whereabouts she was unaware of, from hearing even the sound of her voice, for she was convinced that he did not understand the words, 'and wouldn't it look as if by removing the furniture we were giving up all hope of him making a recovery and were callously leaving him to his own fate? I think it would be best if we tried to keep the room in exactly the same state as before, so that when Gregor returns to us he'll find everything the same and it will be that much easier for him to forget what has happened in the meantime.'

On hearing his mother's words, Gregor realised that the lack of all direct human communication, together with a monotonous life in the midst of his family, must have confused his mind in the course of these last two months, for he could not explain to himself in any other way how he could have seriously wished to have his room cleared out. Did he really want to have his warm room, comfortably furnished with family heirlooms, transformed into a cave in which, admittedly, he would be able to crawl about freely in all directions but at the cost of swiftly and totally forgetting his human past? He was already on the verge of forgetting it, and only his mother's voice, which he had not heard for so long, had brought him to his senses. Nothing should be removed; everything had to stay; he could not do without the beneficial influence of the furniture on his state of mind; and if the furniture prevented him from carrying on with his aimless crawling around, that was no loss, but a great advantage.

But his sister unfortunately thought otherwise; not without some justification, she had grown accustomed to taking on the role, vis-à-vis her parents, of a particularly well-qualified specialist whenever Gregor's affairs were being discussed, and so her mother's advice was now sufficient reason for her to insist on the removal of not only the chest of drawers and desk, which was all she had been planning at first, but of every item of furniture, apart from the indispensable couch. It was, of course, more than childish defiance and the self-confidence so unexpectedly and painstakingly acquired in recent weeks that determined her to make this demand; she had indeed noticed that Gregor needed plenty of room to crawl around in, and there was no sign that he made the slightest use of the furniture. But perhaps a contributory factor was the romantic spirit of girls of her age, which seeks fulfilment at every opportunity and which had now tempted Grete into making Gregor's situation even more horrific, so that she could be of even greater help to him than before. For no one but Grete would ever dare to set foot in a room in which Gregor reigned in solitary state over the bare walls.

And so she would not allow her resolve to be shaken by her mother, who out of sheer nervousness also seemed unsure of herself in that room, and soon fell silent and began doing all she could to help his sister get the chest of drawers out. Now Gregor, if need be, could manage without the chest of drawers, but the desk had to stay. And no sooner had the women left the room, groaning as they flattened themselves against the chest of drawers, than Gregor poked his head from under the couch to see how he might intervene cautiously and with as much tact as possible. But as luck would have it, his mother came back first, while Grete in the adjoining room was clasping the chest of drawers, rocking it unaided to and fro without of course moving it an inch. His mother, however, was not used to the sight of Gregor – looking at him might make her ill – so Gregor reversed in a panic to the other end of the couch, though he was too late to prevent the sheet at the front from swaying a little. That was enough to attract his mother's attention. She stopped in her tracks, stood still for a moment and then went back to Grete.

Although Gregor kept telling himself that nothing out of the ordinary was happening, that only a few pieces of furniture were being moved, he was soon forced to admit that the women's to-ing and fro-ing, their little calls to each other, the scraping of the furniture on the floor, were affecting him like some great turmoil that was being fuelled from all sides, and no matter how firmly he drew in his head and legs and pressed his body against the floor, he knew for certain that he would not be able to stand it much longer. They were clearing out his room; depriving him of everything he loved; they had already carried out the chest of drawers which contained his fretsaw and other tools; now they were prising free the desk that had embedded itself in the floor, at which as a student of commerce, and before that as a schoolboy, in fact ever since his primary-school days, he had always done his homework – and he simply had no more time to verify the good intentions of the two women, whose existence he had in any case almost forgotten, for they were so exhausted that they were now working in silence, and only the heavy shuffling of their feet could be heard.

And so he broke out – in the adjoining room the women were leaning against the desk to catch their breath for a moment – changed direction four times, he really had no idea what to salvage first, then, noticing the picture of the lady draped in nothing but furs where it hung on the otherwise bare wall, he quickly crawled up to it and pressed himself against the glass which held him fast and soothed his hot belly. This picture, at least, which Gregor was now completely covering, was certainly not going to be taken from him. He twisted his head round towards the living-room door to observe the women when they returned.

They had not given themselves much of a rest and were already coming back; Grete had put her arm around her mother and was virtually carrying her. 'So, what shall we take next?' said Grete, and looked about her. And then her eyes met Gregor's as he clung to the wall. It was probably only because her mother was there that she kept her composure, she lowered her face close to her mother's to prevent her from looking around, and said, albeit in a quavering voice and without thinking, 'Come along, hadn't we better go back to the living-room for a moment?' It was clear to Gregor what Grete was up to, she wanted to lead her mother to safety and then chase him down from the wall. Well, just let her try! He was sitting there on this picture and would not part with it. He would sooner fly into Grete's face.

But Grete's words had only served to increase her mother's anxiety; she stepped to one side, caught sight of the huge brown blotch on the flowered wallpaper, and, before it had really dawned on her that it was Gregor she was looking at, cried out in a harsh and screaming voice: 'Oh God, oh God!' and fell across the couch with outstretched arms, as if abandoning everything, and did not stir. 'You, Gregor!' cried his sister with raised fist and piercing eyes. These were the first words she had addressed to him directly since the transformation. She ran into the adjoining room to fetch some smelling-salts to revive her unconscious mother; Gregor wanted to help – he still had time to rescue the picture – but he was stuck to the glass and had to tear himself free; then he too ran into the adjoining room as though he could give his sister some advice, as in the past; but once there he had to stand idly behind her; while rummaging among various little bottles, she turned round and was startled; a bottle fell to the floor and broke; a shard of glass wounded Gregor in the face, some kind of corrosive medicine poured over him; without delaying any longer, Grete now gathered up as many bottles as she could and ran with them in to her mother; she slammed the door behind her with her foot. Gregor was now cut off from his mother, who through his fault was perhaps near to death. He could not open the door for fear of driving away his sister, who had to stay by his mother's side; all he could now do was to wait; and tormented by self-reproach and anxiety, he began to crawl, he crawled over everything, walls, furniture and ceiling, until finally, in his despair, with the whole room starting to spin around him, he fell down onto the middle of the big table.

A short time passed, Gregor lay there limply, silence reigned all around, perhaps that was a good sign. Then the doorbell rang. The maid of course was locked up in her kitchen, and so Grete had to open the door. It was Gregor's father. 'What's happened?' were his first words; Grete's appearance must have told him everything. Grete replied in a muffled voice, with her face presumably pressed against her father's chest, 'Mother fainted, but she's better now. Gregor's broken loose.' 'I knew it,' said his father, 'I kept telling you it would happen, but you women never listen.' It was clear to Gregor that his father had misinterpreted Grete's all-too-brief announcement and assumed that Gregor had been guilty of some act of violence. He now therefore had to try to calm his father down, for he had neither the time nor the means to explain the situation to him. And so he fled to the door of his room and pressed himself against it so that when his father came in from the hallway he could see at once that Gregor had every intention of returning forthwith to his room, that it was unnecessary to drive him back, that he only needed to open the door, at which point he would promptly disappear.

But his father was in no mood to notice such niceties; 'Aha!' he cried on entering, in a tone that suggested simultaneous rage and delight. Gregor drew his head back from the door and lifted it towards his father. He had really not pictured his father the way he now stood there; admittedly, Gregor had been too absorbed recently by his new-found interest in crawling to concern himself, as he used to, with what was going on in the rest of the apartment, and he ought really to have been prepared to find that circumstances had changed. Yes, yes, but could this really be his father? The same man who used to lie wearily buried in bed whenever Gregor set out on a business trip; who greeted him wearing a dressing-gown and reclining in an armchair when he returned in the evening; who was actually hardly capable of getting to his feet, but merely raised his arms to indicate that he was pleased, and who on the rare occasions when the family went for a walk together, on a few Sundays each year and on the major holidays, would always struggle on between Gregor and his mother, who were slow walkers themselves, even slightly more slowly than they, wrapped in his old overcoat, with his crook-handled stick always placed cautiously in front of him, and who, when he wanted to say something, almost invariably stopped and gathered the others around him? Now, however, he held himself erect; he was dressed in a tight-fitting blue uniform with gold buttons, the kind worn by bank messengers; his heavy double chin spilling over the high stiff collar of his jacket; from under his bushy eyebrows his piercing dark eyes had a fresh, alert look; the usually dishevelled white hair had been combed down flat and gleaming on either side of a meticulous parting. He threw his cap, which was adorned with a gold monogram, probably that of some bank, in an arc across the entire room onto the couch, and with the tails of his long livery jacket folded back, his hands in his trouser pockets, he advanced towards Gregor with a grim expression on his face. He himself probably had no idea of what he had in mind; nevertheless, he raised his feet unusually high and Gregor was astonished at the gigantic size of the soles of his boots. But he didn't dwell on that; for he had known from the very first day of his new life that his father believed that the only way to treat him was with the utmost severity. And so he ran on in front of his father, stopping when his father came to a halt, and hurrying forwards again, as soon as his father made a move. In this manner they circled the room several times, without anything decisive occurring, in fact without the whole performance, because of the slow tempo, having the appearance of a chase. So for the time being Gregor kept to the floor, especially as he feared that his father might interpret a flight onto the walls or the ceiling as an act of particular malice on his part. Even so, Gregor had to admit that he would not be able to keep up even this kind of running for long, because for every step his father took he had to execute a whole series of movements. Signs of breathlessness were also becoming apparent, just as in his previous life his lungs had not been wholly reliable. As he now staggered on, hardly keeping his eyes open in order to concentrate entirely on running; not even, in his dazed condition, thinking of any other means of escape but running; and having almost forgotten that the walls were at his disposal, though in this room they were obstructed by elaborately carved furniture bristling with jagged edges and spikes – an object, that had been lightly thrown, suddenly flew right past him, hit the floor and rolled in front of him. It was an apple; a second one came flying right after it; Gregor stopped dead with terror; to continue running was pointless, for his father had decided to bombard him. He had filled his pockets from the fruit bowl on the sideboard and was now, without for the time being taking careful aim, hurling one apple after another. These small red apples rolled about on the floor as if electrified and cannoned into each other. One apple, thrown without force, grazed Gregor's back and glanced off harmlessly. But another, that came flying after it, actually penetrated Gregor's back; Gregor tried to drag himself forward, as if the startling, unbelievable pain might pass with a change of location; but he felt nailed to the spot, and he stretched out his body, with all his senses in a complete blur. The last thing he saw was the door of his room being flung open and his mother rushing out ahead of his screaming sister, in her chemise, as his sister had started undressing her to help her breathe while she was unconscious, and his mother running towards his father, shedding her loosened petticoats one by one on the floor behind her and stumbling over her skirts and flinging herself on him, embracing him in absolute union with him – but now Gregor's sight was beginning to fail – begging him, with hands clasped behind his father's head, to spare Gregor's life.

III

Gregor's severe wound, from which he suffered for more than a month – the apple remained lodged in his flesh as a visible reminder since no one dared to remove it – seemed to have brought home even to his father that Gregor, despite his present sad and repugnant appearance, was a member of the family who should not be treated as an enemy, but that on the contrary family duty required them to swallow their disgust and endure him, simply endure him.

And even though Gregor's wound had caused him to lose for good some of his mobility, and he needed for the time being long, long minutes to traverse his room like an old invalid – crawling above ground was out of the question – he felt fully compensated for this worsening of his condition by the fact that every day around dusk the living-room door, which he was in the habit of watching closely an hour or two beforehand, was thrown open, so that as he lay in the darkness of his room, invisible from the living-room, he could see the whole family at table beneath the lamp, and listen to their conversation, by general consent as it were, and in quite different circumstances than before.

These were of course no longer the animated conversations of the old days, which Gregor had always recalled with some wistfulness in those tiny hotel rooms, when he'd had to throw himself wearily into the damp bedclothes. Things were now mostly very peaceful. Soon after supper his father would fall asleep in his chair; his mother and sister kept reminding each other to be quiet; his mother, leaning far forward under the light, sewed fine linen for a fashion store; his sister, who had taken a job as a salesgirl, was learning shorthand and French in the evenings in the hope of securing a better position later on. Sometimes his father would wake up and, as if unaware that he had been asleep at all, say to his mother: 'You've been doing a lot of sewing again today!', and go right back to sleep, while mother and sister exchanged a weary smile.

With a sort of obstinacy, his father refused to take off his official uniform even in the house; and while his dressing-gown hung idle on the peg, he slept fully clothed in his chair, as if he were permanently ready for duty and awaiting his superior's orders even here. As a result his uniform, which had not been new to start with, lost some of its smartness despite all Gregor's mother and sister could do, and Gregor would often stare all evening long at this garment, covered with stains and gleaming with its constantly polished gold buttons, in which the old man slept in great discomfort and yet at peace.

As soon as the clock struck ten, Gregor's mother tried to wake his father with a gentle word or two and urge him to go to bed, for this was no place to get a proper sleep, which was essential since his father had to report for duty at six o'clock. But with the stubbornness he had acquired since becoming a bank messenger he always insisted on staying longer at table, although he regularly fell asleep and could then only with the greatest difficulty be persuaded to exchange his chair for his bed. No matter how much his mother and sister kept nagging him with mild admonishments, he would go on shaking his head slowly for a quarter of an hour, with his eyes firmly closed and refusing to get up. Gregor's mother plucked at his sleeve, whispered cajoling words in his ear, his sister dropped her homework to come and help her mother, but the effect on his father was nil. He merely sank deeper into his chair. Only when the women grasped him under the armpits would he open his eyes, look from wife to daughter and say: 'What a life. So much for a peaceful old age.' And, leaning on the two women, he would get up awkwardly as if he were the greatest burden to himself, let the women escort him to the door, where, waving them away, he would proceed on his own, while Gregor's mother abandoned her sewing, and his sister her pen in order to run after his father and offer him further assistance.

Who in this overworked and exhausted family had time to worry about Gregor any more than was absolutely necessary? They economised more and more; the maid was finally dismissed; a huge bony cleaning woman with white hair fluttering around her head came mornings and evenings to do the heaviest work; his mother took care of everything else, on top of all her sewing. It even happened that various pieces of family jewellery, which his mother and sister had once been overjoyed to wear at parties and celebrations, were sold, as Gregor discovered one evening from the general discussion about the prices they had fetched. But the chief complaint was always that they could not give up the apartment, which was far too big for their present circumstances, since it was impossible to imagine how Gregor could be moved. But Gregor realised that it was not only concern for him that prevented a move, for it would have been a simple matter to transport him in a suitable crate with a few air-holes; the main reason that prevented the family from moving was rather a feeling of utter hopelessness and the thought that they had been afflicted by a misfortune that none of their friends and relatives had ever suffered. What the world requires of impoverished people they fulfilled to the utmost; his father fetched breakfast for the minor officials at the bank; his mother sacrificed herself making underwear for strangers, his sister ran back and forth behind the counter at her customers' command, but to do any more was beyond the family's power. And the wound in Gregor's back began to hurt all over again when mother and sister, having put his father to bed, now came back, dropped their work, pulled their chairs close together and sat cheek to cheek; when his mother, indicating Gregor's room, said, 'Close that door, Grete'; and when Gregor was again in the dark, while in the next room the women wept together or just stared dry-eyed at the table.

Gregor spent the nights and days almost entirely without sleep. Sometimes he thought that the next time the door opened he would take charge of the family's affairs again just as before; after a long interval the head of the firm and the chief clerk reappeared in his thoughts, together with the other clerks and the apprentices, the exceptionally dim-witted errand-boy, two or three friends from other firms, a chambermaid in a provincial hotel, a fond, fleeting memory, a cashier in a hat shop whom he had courted earnestly but too slowly – they all appeared, intermingled with strangers or people he had already forgotten, but instead of helping him and his family, they were all inaccessible, and he was glad when they disappeared. But at other times he was in no mood to worry about his family, he was consumed by fury at how badly he was being looked after, and although he could think of nothing that he might like to eat, he nonetheless laid plans for gaining access to the larder, to take what was his by rights, even though he wasn't hungry. No longer considering how she might give Gregor a special treat, his sister would shove any old food into his room with her foot, before running off to work every morning and afternoon, and in the evening, regardless of whether the food had merely been picked at or – as was most frequently the case – left completely untouched, she swept it out with a swish of her broom. The cleaning of the room, which she now always attended to in the evenings, could not have been done more speedily. Streaks of dirt lined the walls, heaps of dust and filth lay here and there on the floor. At first, whenever his sister came in, Gregor would station himself in corners of the room that were particularly filthy, implying by this position a sort of reproach. But he could probably have stayed there for weeks without his sister mending her ways; she saw the dirt just as clearly as he did, but had simply decided to leave it there. At the same time she saw to it, with a touchiness that was quite new to her and was indeed affecting the whole family, that the cleaning of Gregor's room should remain her prerogative. On one occasion his mother had undertaken a thorough cleaning of Gregor's room, which she had only managed with the help of several buckets of water – all this dampness, of course, upset Gregor, who lay stretched out on the couch, sullen and immobile – but his mother did not go unpunished. For as soon as his sister noticed the change in Gregor's room that evening, she ran into the living-room, deeply hurt, and despite her mother's imploringly uplifted hands, burst into a fit of sobbing that his parents – his father of course had been startled out of his chair – at first watched in helpless amazement, until they too got excited; his father, to his right, reproached his mother for not leaving the cleaning of Gregor's room to his sister; to his left, on the other hand, he yelled at his sister, saying that never again would she be permitted to clean Gregor's room; while his mother tried to drag his father, who was beside himself with agitation, into the bedroom; his sister, shaken with sobs, hammered the table with her small fists; and Gregor hissed loudly with rage, because nobody thought to close the door and spare him such a spectacle and row.

But even if his sister, worn out by her job, had grown tired of caring for Gregor as she had once done, there was absolutely no need for his mother to take her place, and no reason for Gregor to be neglected. For the cleaning woman was now there. This elderly widow, whose powerful frame had no doubt helped her weather the worst in the course of her long life, had no real horror of Gregor. Without being in the least inquisitive, she had once accidentally opened the door to Gregor's room, and at the sight of Gregor, who, taken completely by surprise, began to run back and forth although no one was chasing him, had stood still in amazement, her hands folded in front of her. From that time on she never failed to open the door a little every morning and every evening to look in at Gregor. At the beginning she even called him over to her with words she probably regarded as friendly, such as, 'Come over here, you old dung-beetle!' or 'Just look at the old dung-beetle!' Gregor never responded to such forms of address but remained motionless where he stood, as if the door had never been opened. If only, instead of allowing this cleaning lady to disturb him pointlessly whenever she felt like it, they had given her orders to clean his room every day! Once, early in the morning – heavy rain, perhaps a sign of approaching spring, was beating against the window-panes – Gregor felt so exasperated when the cleaning woman started prattling again that he turned on her, albeit slowly and like an invalid, as if to attack. Instead of taking fright, however, the cleaning lady merely picked up a chair that was near the door, and as she stood there with her mouth wide open, it was clear that she only intended to shut her mouth when the chair in her hand had come crashing down on Gregor's back. 'You keep your distance, understand?' she said, as Gregor turned around again, and calmly placed the chair back in the corner.

Gregor by now was eating practically nothing. Only when he accidentally went past the food laid out for him would he take a bite as a game, hold it for hours in his mouth and then generally spit it out again. At first he thought it was sadness at the state of his room that was spoiling his appetite, but he had very quickly become reconciled to precisely these changes in his room. His family had got into the habit of putting things in his room that could not be accommodated elsewhere, and there were now many such things, since they had let one room of the apartment to three lodgers. These earnest gentlemen – all three wore beards, as Gregor once observed through a crack in the door – were sticklers for order, not only in their own room but also, now that they were installed as lodgers, throughout the entire apartment and especially in the kitchen. They had no time for useless junk, especially if it was dirty. Besides, they had for the most part brought their own furniture with them. As a result, many things had become superfluous, and though they couldn't be sold, no one wanted to throw them out. All these things ended up in Gregor's room. Likewise the ash bucket and rubbish bin from the kitchen. Whatever was not for the moment being used was simply flung by the cleaning lady, who was always in a great hurry, into Gregor's room; fortunately, Gregor usually saw only the object in question and the hand that held it. Perhaps the cleaning woman intended to retrieve the things when she had the time and opportunity, or throw them all out in one go, but in reality they remained wherever they had been tossed, except when Gregor pushed his way through the junk and set it in motion, at first out of necessity, since there was no other space for crawling, but later with increasing delight, although after such peregrinations he would once again remain motionless for hours on end, tired to death and sad.

As the lodgers sometimes also had their supper at home in the communal living-room, there were certain evenings on which the living-room door stayed shut, but Gregor could do very well without the door being opened, there had after all been quite a few evenings when he had taken no advantage of it being open and had lain, unnoticed by the family, in the darkest corner of his room. But on one occasion the cleaning woman had left the living-room door ajar, and it remained like that when the lodgers came home in the evening and the lamp was lit. They sat down at the head of the table, where in the old days his father, his mother and Gregor had sat, unfolded their napkins and picked up their knives and forks. Gregor's mother promptly appeared in the doorway with a dish of meat, closely followed by his sister with another dish piled high with potatoes. The food gave off thick clouds of steam. The lodgers bent over the plates that were set in front of them as if wishing to examine them before eating, and indeed the one in the middle, whom the others seemed to regard as an authority, sliced a piece of meat while it was still on the dish, obviously to ascertain whether it was tender enough or whether it should not perhaps be sent back to the kitchen. He was satisfied, and mother and sister, who had been watching apprehensively, began to smile with relief.

The family itself ate in the kitchen. Gregor's father, however, before going into the kitchen, entered the living-room and, bowing low, made a tour of the table, cap in hand. The lodgers all stood up and mumbled something into their beards. When they were alone again, they ate in almost complete silence. It seemed odd to Gregor that, among all the multifarious sounds of the meal, he kept picking out the noise of their champing teeth, as though he were being shown that one needed teeth to eat and that even with the finest toothless jaws nothing could be accomplished. 'I do have an appetite,' Gregor said to himself, full of worry, 'but not for those things. Look how these lodgers gorge themselves, while I waste away!'

On this same evening – Gregor could not remember having heard it once in all this time – the sound of violin-playing came from the kitchen. The lodgers had already finished their supper, the one in the middle had produced a newspaper, given each of the others a page, and now, leaning back in their chairs, they were reading and smoking. When the violin began to play, they pricked up their ears, stood up and tiptoed to the door leading into the hall, where they stood in a huddle. Their movements must have been heard in the kitchen, for his father called out, 'Do you find the playing unpleasant, gentlemen? It can be stopped at once.' 'On the contrary,' said the gentleman in the middle, 'wouldn't the young lady like to join us and play in here where it's much more cosy and comfortable?' 'With pleasure,' cried his father, as if he were the violinist. The gentlemen went back into the room and waited. Gregor's father soon came in with the music stand, his mother with the music, his sister with the violin. His sister calmly prepared herself to play; his parents, who had never previously rented out rooms and therefore treated the lodgers with excessive politeness, did not even dare sit down on their own chairs; his father leaned against the door, his right hand inserted between two buttons of his livery jacket; but his mother was offered a chair by one of the gentlemen and sat down where the gentleman had happened to place it, tucked away in a corner.

His sister began to play. Father and mother, from either side, followed attentively the movements of her hands. Gregor, attracted by the playing, had ventured out a little further and already had his head in the living-room. He was hardly surprised that he had recently shown such little consideration for others; such consideration had once been his greatest pride. And now there was even more reason for him to stay out of sight because, as a result of the dust that lay all over his room and blew around at the slightest movement, he too was completely covered in dust; he dragged around with him, on his back and along his sides, lengths of thread, hair and scraps of food; his indifference to everything was much too great for him to turn over on his back and scrub himself clean on the carpet. And in spite of his condition, he was not ashamed to inch out a little further onto the spotless living-room floor.

Not that anyone noticed him. The family was completely

absorbed by the violin-playing; the lodgers on the other hand, who, having stationed themselves, hands in pockets, much too close behind his sister's music stand so that they could all have read the music, which must surely have bothered his sister, soon withdrew, muttering to one another with lowered heads, to the window where they remained, anxiously watched by his father. It really did seem abundantly clear that they were disappointed in their expectation of hearing some beautiful or enjoyable violin-playing, that they were tired of the whole performance, and that it was only out of courtesy that they were permitting their peace to be further disturbed. It was in particular the way they all blew their cigar smoke into the air through the nose and mouth that suggested they were highly stressed. Yet his sister was playing so beautifully. Her face was tilted to one side, her eyes looked sad and searching as they followed the lines of the score. Gregor crawled a little further forward, keeping his head close to the floor so that their eyes might meet. Could he be an animal if music moved him so? He felt as if he were being shown the way to the unknown nourishment that he so craved. He was determined to press forward until he had reached his sister, and suggest by tugging her skirt that she should come into his room with her violin, for no one here appreciated her playing as he would appreciate it. He would never again let her out of his room, at least not as long as he lived; his nightmarish appearance would for once serve some useful purpose; he would be at all the doors of his room at once and spit at his aggressors; his sister, however, would not be compelled to stay with him, but would do so of her own free will; she would sit beside him on the couch and incline her ear towards him, and he would then confide to her that it had been his firm intention to send her to the conservatoire, and that if the catastrophe had not intervened, he would have announced this to everyone last Christmas – Christmas had presumably been and gone? – and would not have listened to any objections. After this declaration his sister would burst into tears of emotion, and Gregor would raise himself to the level of her shoulder and kiss her on the neck which, ever since she started going out to work, she had left bare without a ribbon or collar.

'Herr Samsa!' the middle lodger cried, addressing Gregor's father, and without wasting another word pointed with his index finger at the slowly advancing Gregor. The violin fell silent, the middle lodger with a shake of his head smiled first at his friends, then looked at Gregor again. His father seemed to feel that getting rid of Gregor was for the moment less urgent than reassuring the lodgers, although they were not at all agitated and seemed to derive more pleasure from Gregor than the violin-playing. He hurried over to them and tried with outstretched arms to drive them into their room, and at the same time to block their view of Gregor with his body. Now they really did get a little angry, though it was no longer possible to tell whether this was due to his father's behaviour or because of the dawning realisation that, without their knowledge, they had had such a flatmate as Gregor. They demanded explanations from his father, they themselves now raised their arms, they plucked excitedly at their beards and only slowly retreated to their room. His sister meanwhile had overcome her bewilderment, caused by the abrupt end to her playing, and had suddenly, after holding violin and bow for a time in her limply hanging hands, while continuing to look at the music as if she were still playing, pulled herself together, placed the instrument on her mother's lap, as she sat in her chair fighting for breath with violently pumping lungs, and had run into the adjoining room which the lodgers, driven on by his father, were now approaching more rapidly. Blankets and pillows could be seen flying into the air and falling back onto the bed, guided by his sister's practised hands. Even before the lodgers had reached their room, she had finished making the beds and slipped out. His father seemed once more so overwhelmed by his obstinacy that he forgot every scrap of respect that he should, after all, have shown his tenants. He kept driving them on and on until, already at the bedroom door, the middle lodger stamped his foot with a sound like thunder, and so brought his father to a halt. 'I hereby declare,' he said, raising his hand and looking round for Gregor's mother and sister as well, 'that in view of the repellent conditions prevailing in this apartment and family' – here he spat with sudden resolve onto the floor – 'I intend to vacate this room as of now. I shall not of course pay a penny for the period I have already spent here; I shall on the other hand consider taking action against you with claims that – I assure you – will be very easy to substantiate.' He fell silent and looked straight ahead, as if he were expecting something. And, indeed, his two friends chimed in at once with, 'We also give notice as of now.' Whereupon he seized the door handle and slammed the door.

Gregor's father staggered, groped his way to his chair and slumped onto it; he might have been stretching himself out for his customary evening nap, but the heavy nodding of his head, as if it had lost all support, showed that he was by no means asleep. All this time Gregor had been lying motionless where the lodgers first discovered him. Disappointment at the failure of his plan, but perhaps also the weakness caused by so much fasting, made it impossible for him to move. He feared, with some degree of certainty, that any moment now he was about to suffer a general breakdown, and waited. Not even the violin startled him when it slipped from his mother's trembling fingers, fell off her lap and hit the floor with a resounding clang.

'Dear parents,' said his sister, hitting the table with her hand by way of introduction, 'things cannot go on like this. Maybe you don't realise it, but I do. I will not utter my brother's name in front of this monster, and so all I say is: we must try to get rid of it. We've done everything humanly possible to take care of it, to put up with it, no one can reproach us in the slightest.'

'She's absolutely right,' said his father to himself. His mother, who still could not catch her breath, began to cough into her hand with a hollow sound, and a crazed look came in her eyes.

His sister hurried over to her and put a hand on her forehead. His father, whose thoughts seemed to have crystallised as a result of his sister's words, had sat up straight and was playing with his messenger's cap among the plates that still lay on the table from the lodgers' supper, casting occasional glances at Gregor's motionless form.

'We must try to get rid of it,' his sister now said, addressing only her father, since her mother couldn't hear a word because of her coughing, 'or it will be the death of both of you, I can see it coming. Anyone who works as hard as we all do cannot take this constant torture at home as well. I can't stand it any more.' And she burst into such a violent fit of weeping that her tears flowed onto her mother's face from where she wiped them away with mechanical movements of her hand.

'My child,' said her father sympathetically and with noticeable understanding, 'but what should we do?'

Gregor's sister, who was normally so assured, merely shrugged her shoulders to indicate the helplessness that had come over her during her fit of weeping.

'If he could understand us,' said his father half-questioningly, but his sister, still weeping, waved her hand violently to show that this was unthinkable.

'If he could understand us,' his father repeated, and by closing his eyes comprehended his daughter's conviction that this was impossible, 'then maybe we could come to an agreement with him. But as things are –'

'It has to go,' his sister cried, 'it's the only way, Father. You must try to forget that it's Gregor. Our real downfall is that we've believed it for so long. But how can it be Gregor? If it were Gregor, he would have realised long ago that it isn't possible for humans to live side by side with an animal like that, and would have gone away of his own free will. Then we wouldn't have a brother but would be able to go on living and honour his memory. But as it is, this animal persecutes us, drives away our lodgers, clearly wants to take over the whole apartment and have us sleep in the street. Look, Father,' she suddenly screamed, 'he's at it again!' And in a fit of terror that Gregor found quite incomprehensible, she even abandoned her mother, literally pushing herself off from the chair, as if she would rather sacrifice her mother than remain in Gregor's vicinity, and dashed behind her father who, alarmed solely by her behaviour, also stood up and half-raised his arms in front of her, as if to protect her.

But Gregor hadn't the slightest wish to frighten anyone, especially not his sister. He had merely begun to turn round in order to go back to his room, and that was naturally conspicuous because in his ailing condition he could only execute the difficult manoeuvre with the help of his head, raising and banging it many times against the floor. He stopped in his tracks and looked round. They must have recognised his good intentions; the terror had only been temporary. Now they all looked at him sadly and in silence. His mother was slumped in her chair, her legs stretched out and pressed together, her eyes almost closing from exhaustion; his father and sister sat side by side, his sister had put her arm around their father's neck.

'Perhaps they'll let me turn round now,' Gregor thought, and resumed his labours. He could not help panting with the effort and had to rest from time to time. Not that anyone was harassing him; everything was left to him. When he had completed the turn, he began to crawl back at once in a straight line. He was astonished at the great distance that separated him from his room, and utterly failed to understand how, feeling so weak, he had recently covered the same ground almost without realising it. Concentrating entirely on crawling fast, he hardly noticed that not a single exclamation or word disturbed his progress. Only when he was in the doorway did he turn his head, not all the way, for he felt his neck growing stiff, but enough to see that nothing had changed behind him except that his sister had risen to her feet. His last glimpse was of his mother who had fallen fast asleep.

Hardly was he inside his room than the door was hastily closed, bolted and locked. The sudden noise behind him scared Gregor so badly that his little legs buckled. It was his sister who had been in such a hurry. She had been standing there, upright and waiting, then she had leapt forward nimbly – Gregor had not even heard her coming – and she cried, 'At last!' to her parents as she turned the key in the lock.

'And now?' Gregor asked himself, and looked around in the darkness. He soon discovered that he could no longer move at all. That did not surprise him, in fact he found it unnatural that up until then he had been able to get about on such thin little legs. Otherwise, he felt relatively comfortable. True, he had pains all over his body, but he had the impression that they were gradually growing fainter and fainter and would eventually vanish altogether. By now he could hardly feel the rotten apple in his back and the inflamed area around it, completely covered with soft dust. He recalled his family with tenderness and love. His conviction that he would have to disappear was, if possible, even firmer than his sister's. He remained in this state of vacant and peaceful reflection until the clock tower struck three in the morning. He was still conscious as everything grew brighter outside the window. Then, involuntarily, his head sank right down, and his last breath flowed feebly from his nostrils.

When the cleaning woman came early in the morning – out of sheer energy and impatience, despite frequent requests not to do so, she would slam all the doors with such force that peaceful sleep, once she had arrived, was an impossibility throughout the apartment – she did not at first find anything out of the ordinary as she paid Gregor her usual brief visit. She thought that he was lying there motionless on purpose, pretending that his feelings were hurt; she credited him with boundless intelligence. Because she happened to be holding the long broom, she tried to tickle Gregor with it from the safety of the door. When even this proved unsuccessful she lost patience and gave Gregor a little prod, and it was only when she had shifted him from his place without encountering any resistance that she began to take notice. Having soon become aware of the true state of affairs, she reacted with amazement, whistled softly to herself, did not delay but tore open the bedroom door and yelled into the darkness: 'Take a look at this; it's dead; it's lying there as dead as dead can be!'

The Samsas sat bolt upright in their double bed and took a while to get over the fright the cleaning woman had given them before they finally grasped what she was saying. Then, however, Herr and Frau Samsa got hastily out of bed, each on their own side; Herr Samsa threw the blanket round his shoulders, Frau Samsa emerged in nothing but her nightdress; in this way they entered Gregor's room. Meanwhile the door of the living-room, where Grete had been sleeping since the lodgers moved in, had also opened; she was fully dressed, as if she had not slept at all, an impression that her pale face seemed to confirm. 'Dead?' asked Frau Samsa and looked up enquiringly at the cleaning woman, although she could verify everything for herself and see that it was so without verification. 'I'll say,' said the cleaning woman, and to prove it she gave Gregor's corpse another huge shove to the side with her broom. Frau Samsa made as if to put a restraining hand on the broom but did not do so. 'Well,' said Herr Samsa, 'may God be thanked.' He crossed himself, and the three women followed his example. Grete, without taking her eyes off the corpse, said, 'Just look how thin he was. But then it's ages since he ate anything. The food used to come out again just as it was taken in.' And Gregor's body was indeed completely flat and dry, which could actually only now be observed, since the body was no longer held up by his little legs and there was nothing else to distract the eye.

'Come into our room for a while, Grete,' said Frau Samsa with a wistful smile, and Grete, not without looking back at the corpse, followed her parents into their bedroom. The cleaning woman closed the door and opened the window wide. Despite the early hour the fresh air already had a touch of mildness to it. It was, after all, the end of March.

The three lodgers emerged from their room and stared about them in astonishment for their breakfast; they had been forgotten. 'Where's our breakfast?' the middle lodger sullenly asked the cleaning woman. But she put her finger to her lips and then hastily and silently beckoned the lodgers to follow her into Gregor's room. They did so, and then, with their hands in the pockets of their somewhat shabby jackets, they stood around Gregor's corpse in the now sunlit room.

Then the bedroom door opened, and Herr Samsa appeared in his uniform, with his wife on one arm, his daughter on the other. They all looked as though they had been crying; from time to time Grete pressed her face against her father's arm.

'Get out of my apartment this instant!' said Herr Samsa and pointed to the door, without letting go of the women. 'How do you mean?' said the middle lodger, somewhat taken aback, and smiled a sickly smile. The other two had their hands behind their backs and kept rubbing them together, as if in joyful anticipation of a major quarrel that was bound to end in their favour. 'I mean precisely what I say,' replied Herr Samsa, and, escorted by the two women, marched in a straight line towards the lodger. The latter stood still at first and looked at the floor, as if the thoughts in his head were being rearranged. 'We'll be going, then,' he concluded, and looked up at Herr Samsa as though, in a sudden onset of humility, he were seeking fresh approval for even this decision. Herr Samsa merely gave him several brief nods and glared at him. Whereupon the gentleman did indeed stride immediately into the hallway; his two friends, who for some time had been listening intently and had stopped rubbing their hands, now practically skipped after him, as if afraid that Herr Samsa might reach the hall before them and cut them off from their leader. In the hall all three of them took their hats from the coat rack, pulled their canes from the umbrella stand, bowed silently and left the apartment. With a mistrust that proved totally unfounded, Herr Samsa stepped out onto the landing with the two women;

leaning against the banister, they watched the three gentlemen slowly but steadily descend the long flight of stairs, disappear on each landing at the same bend of the stairwell, then re-emerge a few moments later; the further down they got, the more the Samsa family's interest in them dwindled, and when a butcher's boy, proudly bearing his basket on his head, passed them coming up and then climbed high above them, Herr Samsa and the women soon left the landing, and they all went back, as if relieved, into their apartment.

They decided to spend the day resting and going for a walk; not only had they earned this break from work, they positively needed it. And so they sat down at the table and wrote three letters of apology – Herr Samsa to his superiors at the bank, Frau Samsa to her employers, and Grete to the proprietor of the shop where she worked. While they were writing, the cleaning woman came in to say that she was going because she had finished her morning's work. The three letter-writers merely nodded at first without looking up, but when the cleaning woman still gave no sign of leaving, they looked up in annoyance. 'What is it then?' asked Herr Samsa. The cleaning woman stood smiling in the doorway, as though she had some great good news for the family which, however, she would only disclose if thoroughly quizzed. The almost vertical little ostrich feather in her hat, which had irritated Herr Samsa all the time she had been working for them, swayed gently in all directions. 'Well, what is it you want?' asked Frau Samsa, for whom the cleaning lady still had the most respect. 'It's like this,' answered the cleaning woman and couldn't continue immediately for so much good-natured laughter, 'I mean you mustn't worry about how to clear out that thing in there. It's already taken care of.' Frau Samsa and Grete bent over their letters, as if to continue writing; Herr Samsa, perceiving that the cleaning woman now wished to describe everything in detail, checked her firmly with an upheld hand. But since she was not permitted to tell her story, she remembered she was in a great hurry, called out, obviously insulted: 'Good riddance to all of you,' turned furiously on her heels and left the apartment with a terrible slamming of doors.

'She'll get her notice this evening,' said Herr Samsa, but he received no answer from either his wife or his daughter, for the cleaning woman seemed to have shattered once more their barely regained peace of mind. They got up, went over to the window and stayed there, clasping each other tightly. Herr Samsa turned his chair round to face them, and watched them in silence for a while. Then he called out, 'Come over here, stop brooding over the past. And have a little consideration for me.' The women obeyed him at once, hurried over to him, caressed him and quickly finished their letters.

Then all three of them left the apartment together, something they had not done for months, and took the tram into the country just outside the town. The carriage, in which they were the only passengers, was brightly lit by the warm sun. Leaning back comfortably in their seats, they discussed their prospects for the future, which on closer examination appeared to be far from bad, for all three of them had jobs which, though they had never really discussed it, were entirely satisfactory and boded very well for the future. The greatest immediate improvement in their situation could of course be expected from a simple change of accommodation; they would now take a smaller and cheaper apartment, but better situated and in every way simpler to manage than their present one, which Gregor had found. While they were talking in this way, Herr and Frau Samsa realised at almost the same moment, as they watched their daughter becoming increasingly animated, that recently, despite all the troubles that had turned her cheeks pale, she had blossomed into a beautiful and voluptuous girl. Growing quieter and communicating almost unconsciously through glances, they reflected that it would soon be time to find her a good husband. And it was like a confirmation of their new dreams and good intentions when at the end of the ride their daughter stood up first and stretched her young body.

The Sentence

For F.

It was on a Sunday morning during the loveliest days of spring. Georg Bendemann, a young businessman, was sitting in his room on the first floor of one of the low, lightly built houses that stretched in a long line beside the river, hardly distinguishable from one another except in height and colour. He had just finished a letter to a childhood friend now living abroad, sealed it with playful deliberation, and then, resting his elbow on his desk, looked out of the window at the river, the bridge and the pale green hills on the far bank.

He was thinking about how his friend, dissatisfied with his progress at home, had years before quite literally fled to Russia. Now he was running a business in Petersburg that had begun extremely well but had for a long time been flagging, as his friend complained on his increasingly infrequent visits. So there he was, in a foreign land, wearing himself out to no purpose, the foreign-looking beard imperfectly concealing the face that Georg had known so well since childhood, with its yellow complexion that seemed to indicate some incipient disease. By his own account he had no real contact with the colony of his compatriots out there, and hardly any social life with Russian families either, and was preparing himself for a life of permanent bachelorhood.

What should one write to such a man, who had obviously taken a wrong turn, whom one could pity but not help? Should one advise him to come home perhaps, re-establish his life back here, restore all his old friendships – for nothing stood in the way of that – and rely for the rest on the help of his friends? But that would be tantamount to telling him in the same breath, and the gentler the approach the more offensive it would be, that his efforts so far had failed, that he should abandon them once and for all, that he should come back and let everyone stare wide-eyed at a man who has returned home for good, that only his friends understood such matters and that he was a great baby who must simply do as he was told by these successful friends of his who had stayed at home. And was it even certain that all the pain it would be necessary to inflict would serve any purpose? Perhaps they wouldn't succeed in getting him home at all – he himself admitted that he no longer understood things at home – in which case he would remain abroad in spite of everything, embittered by their suggestions and alienated even further from his friends. If, on the other hand, he followed their advice but fell prey to depression here – not intentionally, of course, but through circumstances – if he failed to get on either with his friends or without them, if he suffered humiliation, and in the end had no real home any more and no friends, might it not have been much better to have stayed abroad just as he was? Was it in such circumstances at all plausible to believe that he would make any progress back here?

For these reasons it was not possible, assuming one wanted to keep up a correspondence with him at all, to inform him of things in the way that one would unhesitatingly inform even the most casual acquaintances. More than three years had passed since his friend had last been home and he attributed this rather feebly to the unstable political situation in Russia, which would apparently permit not even the briefest absence on the part of small businessmen, while hundreds of thousands of Russians were calmly travelling the globe. As it happened, many things had changed for Georg in particular during those three years. The death of Georg's mother, which had occurred about two years earlier, since which time Georg had been living with his old father under the same roof, had in fact reached his friend's ears, and he had expressed his condolences in a letter of such dryness that one could only conclude that mourning over such an event was quite inconceivable when abroad. Since that time, however, Georg had thrown himself into everything, his business included, with greater determination. Perhaps, while his mother was alive, his father had hindered Georg from taking a really active part in the business by insisting on running it in his own way; perhaps, since the death of Georg's mother, his father, though still working in the business, had become more withdrawn; perhaps – and this was highly probable – a series of happy accidents had played a far more important role, at any rate the business had expanded in a most unexpected way during these two years, they had had to take on twice as many staff, the turnover had increased fivefold and further progress was undoubtedly imminent.

The friend, however, had no idea of this change. Earlier, perhaps most recently in that letter of condolence, he had tried to persuade Georg to emigrate to Russia and had elaborated on the prospects that existed for Georg's particular line of business in Petersburg. The figures were minimal compared with the volume of business Georg was now achieving. But Georg had not felt inclined to write to his friend about his business successes, and if he were to do so now in retrospect, it really would have seemed bizarre.

Georg, therefore, always confined himself to writing to his friend about the kind of unimportant events that randomly accumulate in the memory when on a quiet Sunday one has time to reflect. His only wish was to leave undisturbed the mental picture that his friend must have formed of his home town during the long time he had been away and to which he must have become reconciled. Georg had, for example, informed his friend of the engagement of some insignificant man to an equally insignificant girl, until his friend, quite contrary to Georg's intentions, had begun to show an interest in this curious fact.

Georg, however, much preferred to write about things of this nature than to confess that he had himself become engaged a month earlier to a certain Fräulein Frieda Brandenfeld, a girl from a well-to-do family. He often spoke with his fiancée about this friend and the singular relationship they had as correspondents. 'Then he won't be coming to our wedding,' she said, 'and I do have the right to meet all your friends.' 'I don't want to disturb him,' Georg replied. 'Mind you, he probably would come, at least I believe he would, but he would feel self-conscious and hurt, perhaps he would envy me and he'd certainly go back home alone, discontented and incapable of ever shaking off that discontent. Alone – do you know what that means?' 'Yes, but might he not hear about our marriage through other means?' 'There's no way I can prevent that, of course, but it's unlikely if you consider his circumstances.' 'If you have friends like that, Georg, you should never have got engaged at all.' 'Well, we're both to blame there; but even so, I wouldn't want it any other way now.' And when she, breathing heavily as he kissed her, then added, 'No, I'm hurt, I really am,' he decided it would do absolutely no harm to tell his friend the whole story. 'That's the way I am and that's the way he must accept me,' he said to himself. 'I can't fashion myself into someone who might make a more suitable friend for him than I am.'

And in the long letter he wrote that Sunday morning he did

indeed inform his friend of his engagement in the following words: 'I've kept the best news till last. I have become engaged to a certain Fräulein Frieda Brandenfeld, a girl from a well-to-do family who came to live here long after you left, so that you are unlikely to know them. There will be other opportunities to tell you more about my fiancée, just let me say today that I am very happy, and that the only change in our own relationship is that in place of a perfectly ordinary friend you will now have a happy friend. In addition, you have in my fiancée, who sends her warmest regards and will write to you soon herself, a genuine friend of the opposite sex, which for a bachelor is not entirely without insignificance. I know that many things prevent you from visiting us, but wouldn't my wedding provide just the right opportunity to sweep all obstacles aside? But however that may be, make no special allowances and act only as you think fit.'

With this letter in his hand and his face turned to the window, Georg had continued to sit for a long time at his desk. An acquaintance, who had greeted him from the street below, received hardly even a vacant smile in response.

At last he put the letter in his pocket and stepped from his room across and along a small corridor into his father's room, where he had not been for months. Nor was there any particular need for him to go there, for he was in constant contact with his father at the office, they took their midday meal together in a restaurant, and though they made separate arrangements for supper, they would usually, when Georg was not out with friends, which was most frequently the case, or more recently visiting his fiancée, sit up for a while, each with his newspaper, in the living-room they shared.

Georg was astonished at how dark his father's room was even on this sunny morning. What a shadow it cast, that high wall, rising up beyond the narrow courtyard. His father was sitting by the window in a corner that was adorned with various mementos of Georg's late mother, reading a newspaper which he held up to his eyes at an angle in an attempt to compensate for some weakness of vision. On the table stood the remains of his breakfast, not much of which appeared to have been consumed.

'Ah, Georg!' said his father, and rose at once to meet him. His heavy dressing-gown opened as he walked, the flaps fluttering round him. 'My father is still a giant,' Georg said to himself.

'It's unbearably dark here,' he said.

'Yes, it is dark,' his father replied.

'You shut the window too?'

'I prefer it like that.'

'It's really warm outside,' said Georg, as if following up his earlier remark, and sat down.

His father cleared away the breakfast things and put them on a cabinet.

'I just wanted to tell you,' Georg continued, lost in thought as he followed the old man's movements, that I've sent word of my engagement to Petersburg after all. He drew the letter a little way out of his pocket and let it slip back again.

'Why Petersburg?' his father asked.

'To my friend, of course,' said Georg, and tried to catch his father's gaze. – 'He's quite different in the office,' he thought, 'just look at him sitting here so broad-shouldered, with his arms folded across his chest.'

'Quite. Your friend,' his father said with emphasis.

'You remember, Father, that I wanted at first to keep my engagement from him. Out of consideration for his feelings, for no other reason. You know yourself how difficult he is. I told myself that he could find out about my engagement from some other source, even though, given his isolated life, that's hardly likely – I can't prevent that – but I definitely didn't want him to hear about it from me.'

'And now you've changed your mind?' his father enquired, laying his large newspaper on the window-sill, and on top of that his spectacles which he covered with his hands.

'Yes, now I've changed my mind. If he is a true friend, I said to myself, then my being happily engaged will make him happy too. That's why I no longer had any hesitation in telling him. But I wanted to tell you before I posted the letter.'

'Georg,' his father said, and tautened his toothless mouth, 'listen to me! You've come to me with this matter because you want to talk it over. That certainly does you credit. But it's meaningless, it's worse than meaningless, if you don't now tell me the whole truth. I have no wish to stir up matters that don't belong here. Since the death of our dear mother certain rather distasteful things have occurred. Perhaps the time will come to speak of them too, perhaps it will come sooner than we think. A fair amount escapes me at work, it might not be intentionally hidden from me – I'm certainly not trying to suggest that things are being hidden from me – I am no longer strong enough, my memory is going, I can no longer keep track of so many different matters. It's partly nature taking its course, and it's partly because Mummy's death has affected me much more than you. – But since we are discussing this matter, this letter, I beg you, Georg, not to deceive me. It's a trifle, it's not worth bothering about, so don't deceive me. Does this friend in Petersburg really exist?'

Georg stood up in embarrassment. 'Let's leave my friends out of this. A thousand friends can never take the place of my father. You know what I think? You're not taking enough care of yourself. But old age demands its due. I can't do without you in the business, you know that very well, but if the business were to threaten your health, I'd shut it down tomorrow once and for all. I'm not having that. We must introduce a change in your lifestyle. A radical change. You sit here in the dark, whereas you could have good light in the living-room. You peck at your breakfast instead of tucking in. You sit with the window shut, and the air would do you so much good. No, Father! I shall get the doctor to come and we'll follow his advice. We'll swap rooms, you can take the front room, I'll move in here. It won't cause any upset for you because we'll move all your things over too. But there's time for all that, just lie down in bed for a while, what you really need is rest. Come, I'll help you get undressed, I can, you'll see. Or would you like to go to the front room at once, in which case you can lie down in my bed for a bit. In fact that would be a very sensible thing to do.'

Georg was standing close by his father, who had let his head of shaggy white hair sink onto his chest.

'Georg,' said his father softly, without moving.

Georg immediately knelt down beside his father, he saw the dilated pupils of his father's weary face staring at him from the corners of his eyes.

'You have no friend in Petersburg. You've always been a joker, and haven't spared even me with your jokes. Why should you have a friend there of all places? I simply don't believe it.'

'Just cast your mind back, Father,' Georg said, and lifted his father out of his chair and, because he was so frail, pulled off his dressing-gown, 'it must have been almost three years ago that my friend was here on a visit. I can still recall that you didn't particularly like him. On at least two occasions I told you that he wasn't here, although he was sitting in my room at the time. I could well understand your dislike of him, my friend does have his peculiarities. But then there were occasions when you got on perfectly well with him. I felt really proud of the fact that you were listening to him, nodding your head and asking him questions. If you think hard, you're bound to remember. He used to tell us incredible stories of the Russian Revolution. How, for example, during a riot on a business trip to Kiev, he had seen a priest on a balcony cut a large bleeding cross into the palm of his hand, raise that hand and call out to the crowd. You've even told the story yourself from time to time.'

In the meantime Georg had managed to lower his father into the chair again and carefully remove both his socks and the knitted trousers he wore over his linen underpants. At the sight of the not-especially-clean underwear, he reproached himself for having neglected his father. One of his duties should surely have been to check that his father changed his underwear. He had not yet really discussed with his fiancée how they were going to arrange his father's future, for they had tacitly assumed that he would stay on in the old apartment by himself. But now, all of a sudden, Georg was adamant that he would take his father with him into his new home. It almost looked, on closer inspection, as though the care his father would be given there might come too late.

He carried his father in his arms to the bed. A terrible feeling came over him when he noticed, during those two or three paces, that his father was playing with the watch-chain on his chest. He was holding onto the watch-chain so tightly that Georg was unable for the moment to put his father to bed.

Once he was in bed, however, all seemed well. He covered himself up on his own and then pulled the blanket unusually high across his shoulders. He looked up at Georg in a not unfriendly manner.

'You do remember him, don't you?' Georg asked, and nodded at him with encouragement.

'Am I well covered up now?' asked his father, as if he couldn't see whether his feet were adequately covered.

'You like it in bed, then,' said Georg, and tucked him in more thoroughly.

'Am I well covered up?' his father asked once more, and seemed to await the answer with special interest.

'Don't worry, you're well covered up.'

'No!' shouted his father, crashing the answer down on the question, and flung back the blanket with such force that it completely unfolded for a moment as it flew through the air. He was standing erect on the bed, with a single hand pressed lightly against the ceiling. 'You wanted to cover me up, I know you did, you good-for-nothing, but I'm not covered up yet. And even if I'm not as strong as I was, I've enough strength for you, more than enough. Of course I know your friend. A son after my own heart, he'd have been. That's why you've been deceiving him all these years. Why else? Do you think I haven't wept for him? Isn't that why you lock yourself in the office, not to be disturbed, the boss is busy – purely in order to write your lying little letters to Russia. But fortunately, no one needs to teach your father to see through his son. And now that you thought you'd got the better of him, got the better of him so that you're able to plant your backside on him and he doesn't move, my high-and-mighty son decides to get married!'

Georg gazed up at the terrifying vision of his father. His friend in Petersburg, whom his father suddenly knew so well, affected him as never before. He pictured him lost in far-off

Russia. He saw him at the door of his empty, plundered shop. Scarcely able to stand among his smashed shelves, the mangled merchandise and the falling gas brackets. Why had he felt compelled to go so far away!

'Look at me, will you!' his father shouted, and Georg ran almost absent-mindedly over to the bed in an effort to comprehend everything, but stopped halfway.

'Because she lifted her skirts,' his father began to pipe, 'because she lifted her skirts like this, the filthy bitch,' and by way of illustration he lifted his nightshirt so high that the scar from his war years could be seen on his upper thigh, 'because she lifted her skirts like this and this and this, you went for her, and in order to have your way with her undisturbed, you desecrate your mother's memory, betray your friend and stick your father into bed so that he can't move. But can he move, or can't he?'

And there he stood, completely unsupported, kicking his legs. He was radiant with insight.

Georg stood in a corner, as far from his father as possible. A long time ago he had firmly resolved to observe everything with the greatest of attention, in order not to be ambushed in any devious way, either from behind or from above. Once more he remembered that long-forgotten decision and forgot it, like a short thread being drawn through the eye of a needle.

'But your friend has not been betrayed!' his father shouted, and his wagging forefinger confirmed it. 'I've been representing him right here.'

'Play-actor!' Georg couldn't help calling out, realised immediately the harm this caused, and with staring eyes bit his tongue so hard that he doubled up in pain.

'Of course I've been play-acting! Play-acting! That's just the word for it! What other consolation was left to your old widowed father? Tell me – and for the time it takes to answer, you shall still be my living son – what else was left to me, in my back room, persecuted by disloyal staff, old to my very bones. And my son went on his exultant way through the world, clinched deals that I had set up, fell over himself with glee, walked past his father with the inscrutable face of a man of honour, and left! Do you think I didn't love you, I who gave you your being?'

'He's about to lean forward,' Georg thought, 'if only he'd fall and smash himself to pieces!' These words went hissing through his head.

His father leaned forward, but did not fall. As Georg, contrary to his father's expectation, did not approach, he straightened up again.

'Stay where you are, I don't need you! You think you still have the strength to come over here and are merely holding back because you want to. Well, don't deceive yourself! I'm still the stronger by far. On my own I might have had to give way, but your mother passed on her strength to me, I've formed a splendid alliance with your friend, I've got a list of your clients here in my pocket!'

'He's even got pockets in his nightshirt!' Georg said to himself, thinking that with this remark he could make his father look foolish in the eyes of the entire world. He only thought it for a fraction of a second, because he kept forgetting everything.

'Take your fiancée's arm and try coming near me! I'll soon swat her away from your side, just you wait and see!'

Georg made a face, as though he did not believe it. His father merely nodded towards Georg in the corner, protesting all the while the truth of what he had said.

'How you amused me today when you came and asked

whether you should write to your friend about the engagement. He knows everything, you foolish boy, he knows everything! I wrote to him myself, because you forgot to take away my writing things. That's why he hasn't come here for years, he knows everything a hundred times better than you, he screws up your unread letters in his left hand, while holding up mine to be read in his right!'

In his enthusiasm he waved an arm above his head. 'He knows everything a thousand times better!' he shouted.

'Ten thousand times!' said Georg, intending to mock his father, but before the words had left his lips they had taken on a deadly serious tone.

'For years I've been waiting for you to come along with that question! Do you think I care about anything else? Do you think I read newspapers? There!' And he threw Georg a page that had somehow found its way into his bed. An old paper, whose name was completely unknown to Georg.

'The time it's taken you to reach maturity! Your mother had to die, she was not to witness the happy day, your friend is going to rack and ruin in his Russia, even three years ago his face was yellow enough for the scrap heap, and I, well, you see how things are with me. You've eyes enough for that!'

'So you've been lying in wait for me!' cried Georg.

In a sympathetic tone his father said casually, 'You probably meant to say that before. But now it's no longer relevant.'

And in a louder voice: 'So now you know what else there was apart from you, till now you've only known about yourself! You were an innocent child, it's true, but truer still – you were the devil incarnate! – Therefore know: I hereby sentence you to death by drowning!'

Georg felt himself driven from the room, the crash with which his father fell on the bed behind him still ringing in his ears. On the stairs, which he took at a rush as though speeding down an incline, he startled his maid who was going up to tidy the apartment after the night. 'Jesus!' she cried, and covered her face with her apron, but he was already gone. He shot out of the gate, across the road, driven on towards the water. He clutched the railings as a starving man clutches food. He vaulted over them like the accomplished gymnast he had been in his youth, much to his parents' pride. Still holding on with a weakening grip, between the bars of the railings he caught sight of a bus that would easily smother the noise of his fall, and called softly, 'Dear parents, I have always loved you,' and let himself drop.

A quite endless stream of traffic was just crossing the bridge.

Give up!

It was very early in the morning, the streets clean and deserted, I was walking to the station. As I compared a tower clock with my watch, I saw that it was already much later than I had thought, I had to hurry, the shock of this discovery made me uncertain of the way, I was not yet very well acquainted with the town, fortunately there was a policeman nearby, I ran up to him and breathlessly asked him the way. He smiled and said: 'You are asking *me* the way?' 'Yes,' I said, 'since I cannot find it myself.' 'Give up, give up,' he said, and turned away with a great sweep, like people who want to be alone with their laughter.

Outside the Law

Outside the Law stands a doorkeeper. To this doorkeeper comes a man from the country and requests admittance to the Law. But the doorkeeper says that he cannot admit him just now. The man reflects and then asks whether he might be admitted at a later date. 'Possibly,' says the doorkeeper, 'but not now.' Since the door to the Law stands open as always and the doorkeeper steps aside, the man bends down to look beyond the door into the interior. When the doorkeeper notices, he laughs and says: 'If it tempts you so, try to enter despite my ban. But mark my words: I am powerful. And I am only the lowest doorkeeper. From hall to hall there are other doorkeepers, each more powerful than the last. The mere sight of the third is more than even I can bear.' The man from the country had not expected such difficulties; after all, he thinks, the Law should always be accessible to everyone, but as he now takes a closer look at the doorkeeper in his fur coat, at his great pointed nose, his long, thin, black Tartar beard, he decides that he will in fact wait until he receives permission to enter. The doorkeeper gives him a stool and lets him sit down to one side of the door. There he sits for days and years. He makes many attempts to be admitted and wearies the door-keeper with his entreaties. The doorkeeper often interrogates him a little, asks him about his home and many other things, but they are uninterested questions, such as the high and mighty ask, and in the end he always tells him that he cannot yet be admitted. The man, who has equipped himself with many things for his journey, uses all that he has, however valuable, in order to bribe the doorkeeper. The latter accepts it all, but says in doing so: 'I only accept lest you should think you'd left some stone unturned.' During these many years the man observes the doorkeeper almost uninterruptedly. He forgets the other doorkeepers, and this first one seems to him the only obstacle barring his admission to the Law. He curses his misfortune, fiercely and out loud in the early years, later, as he grows old, he only mutters under his breath. He becomes childish, and, since during the long years of studying the doorkeeper he has also got to know the fleas in his fur collar, he also begs the fleas to help him change the doorkeeper's mind. Eventually his sight begins to fail, and he does not know whether it is really growing darker around him or whether his eyes are deceiving him. But he does now discern in the darkness a radiance that streams inextinguishably from the door of the Law. Now he has not much longer to live. Before he dies, all the experiences of this entire time gather in his mind to form one question that he has not yet asked the doorkeeper. He beckons to him, for he can no longer raise his now-stiffening body. The doorkeeper has to bend right down to him, since the difference in height has changed very much to the man's disadvantage. 'What do you want to know now?' the doorkeeper asks, 'you are insatiable.' 'Everyone strives to reach the Law,' says the man, 'so how is it that in all these years no one but me has demanded admittance?' The doorkeeper realises that the man is at his end, and, in order to reach his failing hearing, yells at him: 'No one else could have gained admittance here, for this entrance was intended for you alone. I shall now go and close it.'

A Country Doctor

I was in a great quandary: I had an urgent journey to make; a gravely ill patient awaited me in a village ten miles away; a blizzard filled the wide expanse between us; I had a cart, a light one with large wheels, just right for our country lanes; bundled up in my fur coat, instrument bag in hand, I was standing in the yard all ready to go; but I had no horse, no horse. My own horse had perished the previous night from overexertion in this icy winter; my servant-girl was now running round the village trying to borrow a horse; but it was hopeless, I knew it, and I stood around aimlessly, with more and more snow piling on top of me, becoming more and more immobile. The girl appeared at the gate alone, and waved her lamp; of course, who would lend a horse at such a time for such a journey? I strode once more across the courtyard; I could think of no solution; distracted and tormented I kicked against the rotten door of the pigsty which had not been used for years. It flew open and banged to and fro on its hinges. Warmth emerged, and a smell like that of horses. A dim stable lantern swung from a rope inside. A man, crouching in the low-roofed shed, raised his candid blue-eyed face. 'Shall I harness the horses?' he asked, crawling out on all fours. I could think of nothing to say and merely stooped down to see what else was in the sty. The servant-girl stood by my side. 'You never know what you've got in your own house,' she said, and we both laughed. 'Gee-up, brother, gee-up, sister!' the groom cried, and two horses, powerful beasts with mighty flanks, legs tucked in and lowering their shapely heads like camels, pushed their way, by the sheer power of their twisting rumps, out of the doorway which they filled completely. Next moment, they were standing upright, high on their long legs, their bodies emitting a dense steam. 'Give him a hand,' I said, and the willing girl ran to pass the harness to the groom. No sooner had she reached his side, however, than the groom flings his arms around her and clamps his face to hers. She screams and takes refuge by my side; the red imprint of two rows of teeth was sunk into the girl's cheek. 'You brute,' I yell furiously, 'do you want a whipping?' but then remember at once that he is a stranger; that I do not know where he comes from and that he is volunteering his help while everyone else has let me down. As if he knew what I was thinking, he takes no offence at my threat but, still busy with the horses, merely turns once in my direction. 'Get in,' he says, and sure enough: all is ready. I make a mental note that I've never before ridden behind so fine a pair of horses, and climb cheerfully in. 'I shall drive, though, you don't know the way,' I say. 'Of course,' he says, 'I'm not coming at all, I'm staying with Rosa.' 'No,' screams Rosa, and with an accurate foreboding of her inevitable fate she runs into the house; I hear the door chain rattle as she draws it tight; I hear the lock snap shut; I also see her turn off the lights in the hall, and then, racing through the other rooms, all the other lights, to avoid being found. 'You're coming with me,' I tell the groom, 'or I won't go, however urgent the journey is. I've no intention of handing over the girl to you as payment for the ride.' 'Get a move on there!' he says; he claps his hands; the cart is whisked away like timber caught by the current; I just have time to hear the door of my house burst and splinter under the groom's assault, before my eyes and ears are filled with a mighty rushing that penetrates all my senses equally. But even that lasts only a moment, for, as if my patient's courtyard had opened up directly in front of my own gate, I am already there; the horses are waiting quietly; the snow has stopped falling; moonlight all around; the patient's parents come hurrying out of the house; his sister behind them; I am almost lifted out of the cart; I can't make any sense of their confused talk; the air in the sick-room is barely breathable; the neglected stove is smoking; I shall open the window; but first I want to see the patient. Thin, without fever, neither cold nor warm, shirtless and with vacant eyes, the young man raises himself up beneath the quilt, clings to my neck, whispers into my ear: 'Doctor, let me die.' I look about me; nobody heard; the parents are leaning forward, silently awaiting my verdict; the sister has brought a chair for my bag. I open the bag and search among my instruments; the boy keeps reaching out towards me from his bed to remind me of his request; I pick up a pair of forceps, examine them by the light of the candle and put them back again. 'Yes,' I reflect profanely, 'in cases like this the gods lend a hand, send along the missing horse, add a second for the sake of speed, and for good measure provide the groom –' Only now do I think of Rosa; what shall I do, how shall I save her, how can I drag her out from under that groom, ten miles away, with unman-ageable horses harnessed to my cart. These horses, who have somehow loosened the reins; they push open the windows, I've no idea how, from the outside; each has stuck its head through a window and, unperturbed by the family's screams, contemplate the patient. 'I'll drive straight back home,' I reflect, as if the horses were summoning me to start, but I allow the sister, who thinks I am overcome by the heat, to remove my fur coat. A glass of rum is set before me, the old man pats me on the shoulder, the sacrifice of his treasure justifies the familiarity. I shake my head; I would feel sick within the narrow confines of the old man's intellect; that is the only reason why I refuse the drink. The mother stands by the bed and beckons me over; I obey and, while one horse neighs loudly at the ceiling, lay my head against the boy's chest, who shudders at the touch of my wet beard. What I already knew is confirmed: the boy is healthy, with slightly poor circulation, saturated with coffee by his anxious mother, but healthy and best kicked out of bed at once. I am no world reformer and let him lie there. I'm employed by the local authority and do my duty to the limit, almost beyond the limit. Badly paid, I am nonetheless generous and helpful to the poor. I have to take care of Rosa too, then the boy may be right, and I too shall wish to die. What am I doing here in this endless winter! My horse has perished, and no one in the village will lend me theirs. I have to drag my team out of the pigsty; if they did not happen to be horses, I would have to ride sows. That's the way it is. And I nod to the family. They know nothing about it, and if they did they wouldn't believe it. Writing prescriptions is easy, but communicating with people is hard. Well, this seems to be the end of my visit, once again I've been summoned for nothing, I'm used to it, with the help of my night-bell the entire district torments me, but having this time to abandon Rosa as well, that lovely girl who for years, barely noticed by me, has been living in my house – this sacrifice is too great, and I must somehow justify it in my mind with subtle sophistry if I am not to let fly at this family, who with the best will in the world cannot bring Rosa back to me. But as I close my bag and gesture for my fur coat, as the family stands there together, the father sniffing at the glass of rum in his hand, the mother, probably disappointed in me – just what do people expect? – tearfully biting her lips, and the sister waving a blood-soaked towel, I am somehow prepared, under the circumstances, to admit that the young man may be ill after all. I go to him, he smiles at me as if I were bringing him the most nourishing of broths – ah, now both horses are neighing; the noise, ordained from on high, is probably intended to make the examination easier – and I find: yes, the boy is ill. In his right side, in the region of the hip, there was a gaping wound as big as the palm of my hand. Pink, in many shades, dark in the depths, paler towards the edges, soft-grained, the blood welling unevenly, gaping like the surface of a mine. From a distance, that is. A closer inspection reveals a further complication. A sight to make anyone whistle beneath their breath. Worms, the length and thickness of my little finger, rosy with their own blood as well as being spattered with it, firmly attached to the inside of the wound, are writhing upwards into the light with their little white heads and many legs. Poor boy, there's no hope for you. I have discovered your great wound; this flower in your side is destroying you. The family is happy, it sees me occupied; the sister informs her mother, the mother the father, and the father informs several guests who, balancing with outstretched arms, tiptoe in through the moonlight of the open door. 'Will you save me?' the boy whispers with a sob, utterly dazzled by the life in his wound. That's the way people are in my district. Always demanding the impossible of a doctor. They have lost the ancient faith; the priest sits at home and picks his vestments apart, one after the other; but the doctor, with his sensitive surgical hands, is expected to accomplish everything. Be that as it may: I didn't offer my services; if you misuse me for religious purposes, I'll put up with that too; what more can I ask for, an old country doctor bereft of my servant-girl! And they come, the family and the village elders, and they strip me; a school choir led by their teacher stands in front of the house and sings this verse to the simplest of melodies:

Strip him, then he'll heal us,
And if he does not, kill him!
He's only a doctor, only a doctor.

There I stand stripped of my clothes and, my fingers in my beard and my head bowed, gaze calmly at the people. I am utterly composed and superior to them all, and remain so, though it doesn't help me, for now they seize me by the head and feet and carry me to the bed. They lay me down against the wall, on the side where the wound is. Then they all leave the room; the door is closed; the singing dies away; clouds pass across the moon; the bedclothes lie warmly about me; the horses' heads sway in the window openings like shadows. 'You know,' says a voice in my ear, 'I have very little faith in you. After all, you only drifted in from somewhere, you didn't get here on your own two feet. Instead of helping, you're cramping me on my deathbed. I'd like most of all to scratch your eyes out.' 'Correct,' I say, 'it's a disgrace. But I am a doctor. What am I to do? Believe me, it won't be easy for me either.' 'You expect me to put up with that excuse? Ah well, I suppose I'll have to. I always have to put up with things. I came into the world with a fine wound; that's all I was endowed with.' 'My young friend,' I say, 'your problem is that you lack an overview. I, who have been in every sick-room, far and wide, say to you: your wound is not so bad. Inflicted by two slanting blows of the axe. There are many who offer their sides and hardly hear the axe in the forest, let alone hear it coming closer to them.' 'Is that really so, or are you deluding me in my fever?' 'That's how it is, take a medical officer's word for it as you pass away.' And he took it and fell silent. But now it was time to think about how to save myself. The horses still stood faithfully in their places. Clothes, fur coat and bag were swiftly bundled together; I didn't want to waste time getting dressed; if the horses raced as they had on the way here, I would, so to speak, be jumping out of this bed into mine. Obediently, one horse drew back from the window; I hurled my bundle into the cart; the fur coat flew too far, it clung to a hook by a single sleeve. Good enough. I swung myself onto the horse – the reins trailing loosely along, one horse barely attached to the other, the cart meandering behind, and last of all the fur coat in the snow. 'Gee up! Look lively!' I cried, but the ride was not lively; slowly, like old men, we moved through the snowy wasteland; for a long time we could hear behind us the children's new but erroneous song:

> *O be joyful, all you patients,*
> *The doctor's laid in bed beside you!*

I shall never reach home like this; my flourishing practice is lost; a successor is robbing me, but to no purpose, since he cannot replace me; the repugnant groom wreaks havoc in my house; Rosa is his victim; I refuse to think of the consequences. Naked, exposed to the frost of this most unhappy era, with an earthly cart and unearthly horses, I, an old man, am adrift. My fur coat hangs from the back of the cart, but I cannot reach it, and not one among my sprightly rabble of patients lifts a finger to help. Betrayed! Betrayed! Once you've responded to the night-bell's false alarm – the mistake can never be rectified.

The Bridge

I was stiff and cold, I was a bridge, I lay across an abyss. My toes dug deep on one side, my hands on the other, I had sunk my teeth into crumbling clay. The tails of my coat fluttered at my sides. The icy trout stream roared below me. No tourist strayed to these rugged heights, the bridge was not yet marked on any map. Thus I lay and waited; I had to wait. Without collapsing, no bridge, once erected, can cease to be a bridge. Once, towards evening, whether it was the first or thousandth I cannot tell, my thoughts were always confused and always going round in circles – towards evening in the summer, with the roar of the stream now deeper, I heard human footsteps. Come to me, to me. Stretch yourself, bridge, prepare yourself, girder without rail, bear the one entrusted to you, steady unobtrusively his uncertain steps, but if he stumbles, show your mettle and like a mountain god hurl him to the other side. He came, he tapped me with the iron spike of his stick, with which he then lifted my coat-tails and folded them about me, he plunged his spike into my bushy hair and let it rest there for quite some time, doubtlessly gazing all around him. But then – I was just following him in reverie over mountain and valley – he jumped with both feet onto the middle of my body. I shuddered with wild pain, utterly uncomprehending. Who was it? A child? A gymnast? A daredevil? A suicide? A tempter? An annihilator? And I turned over to look at him. A bridge turns over! I had not yet fully turned, when I began to fall; I fell, and in a moment I was ripped apart and impaled on the sharp stones that had always gazed so peacefully up at me out of the raging waters.

The Hunter Gracchus

Two boys were sitting on the harbour wall playing dice. On the steps of a monument a man was reading a newspaper in the shadow of the sword-brandishing hero. A girl was filling her pail at the fountain. A fruit-seller was lying beside his wares, looking out across the lake. Two men could be seen through the gaping door and window of a tavern, drinking wine. The proprietor was sitting at a table in the front, dozing. A bark glided silently, as if borne over the water, into the little harbour. A man in a blue smock climbed ashore and pulled the rope through the rings. Behind the boatman two other men in dark silver-buttoned coats carried a bier draped with a great tasselled cloth of flower-patterned silk, under which a man was apparently lying. Nobody on the quayside bothered about the newcomers, even when they lowered the bier to wait for the boatman still busy with his ropes, nobody approached, nobody asked them a question, nobody gave them a closer look. The boatman was delayed a little longer by a woman who now appeared on deck with flowing hair and a child at her breast. Then he came up and indicated a yellowish two-storeyed house that rose abruptly on the left close by the water, the bearers took up their burden and carried it through the low but gracefully pillared door. A little boy opened the window just in time to see the group disappear into the house, then hastily shut the window again. Now the door was shut too, it was of heavy oak and carefully constructed. A flock of doves which had been flying round the belfry alighted in front of the house. As if their food were stored within, the doves gathered in front of the door. One of them flew up to the first floor and pecked at the window-pane. They were brightly coloured, well-looked-after, lively creatures. The woman on the boat flung grain to them in a great arc, they ate it up and flew across to the woman. An old man in a black-ribboned top-hat came down one of the narrow and very steep lanes that led to the harbour. He cast careful looks about him, everything worried him, the sight of some rubbish in a corner made him grimace, fruit skins were lying on the steps of the monument, as he passed he swept them down the lane with his stick. He knocked at the pillared door, at the same time taking the top-hat from his head with his black-gloved right hand. The door was opened at once, some fifty little boys lined up opposite one another in the long entrance hall and bowed. The boat-man came down the stairs, greeted the gentleman, led him up, escorted him round the delicately built loggia that encircled the courtyard and, while the boys thronged after them at a respectful distance, they both entered a cool, large room at the back of the building, from which no other house but merely a bare grey-black wall of rock could be seen. The bearers were busy setting up and lighting several long candles at the head of the bier; yet these did not give off light, but only disturbed the shadows which till then had been immobile, and made them flicker over the walls. The cloth covering the bier had been thrown back. A man lay there with hair and beard wildly matted, rather like a hunter, with suntanned skin. He lay there motionless, his eyes closed, apparently without breathing, yet only the surroundings indicated that he was perhaps dead.

The gentleman stepped up to the bier, laid his hand on the recumbent figure's forehead, then knelt down and prayed. The boatman made a sign to the bearers to leave the room, they went out, drove away the boys who had gathered outside, and shut the door. But even that did not seem to be quiet enough for the gentleman, he looked at the boatman, who understood and vanished through a side-door into the next room. The man on the bier immediately opened his eyes, smiled painfully, turned his face towards the gentleman and said, 'Who are you?' The gentleman rose from his kneeling position without any sign of surprise and replied, 'The burgomaster of Riva.' The man on the bier nodded, pointed to a chair with a feeble movement of his outstretched arm, and said, after the burgomaster had accepted the invitation: 'I knew that, of course, Mr Burgomaster, but initially I always find I have forgotten everything, everything is in a whirl and it is better for me to ask, even if I know everything. You too probably know that I am the Hunter Gracchus.' 'Certainly,' said the burgomaster, 'your arrival was announced to me during the night. We had been asleep for a long time. Then getting on for midnight my wife cried, "Salvatore" – that's my name – "look at that dove at the window." It really was a dove, but as big as a cockerel. It flew up to my ear and said: "The dead Hunter Gracchus is coming tomorrow, receive him in the name of the city." ' The hunter nodded and licked his lips with the tip of his tongue: 'Yes, the doves fly on ahead of me. But do you think, Mr Burgomaster, that I should remain in Riva?' 'That I cannot yet say,' replied the burgomaster. 'Are you dead?' 'Yes,' said the Hunter, 'as you can see. Many years ago, it must have been a great many years, I fell from a rock in the Black Forest – that is in Germany – when I was hunting a chamois. Since then I have been dead.' 'But you are also alive,' said the burgomaster. 'To a certain extent,' said the hunter, 'to a certain extent I am also alive. My death ship went off course, a wrong turn of the wheel, a moment's lack of concentration from the helmsman, distracted by my lovely native country, I don't know the cause, I only know that I remained on earth and that ever since, my boat has been sailing earthly waters. So

I, who merely wished to live among my mountains, travel since my death through all the countries of the earth.' 'And you have no link with the hereafter?' asked the burgomaster with furrowed brow. 'I am forever,' replied the hunter, 'on the great stairway that leads up to it. I drift around that infinitely wide and open stairway, sometimes at the top, sometimes at the bottom, sometimes on the right, sometimes on the left, always in motion. But when I soar up as high as I can and already see the shining gate above me, I wake up on my old boat, still stranded forlornly on some earthly stretch of water. The fundamental error of my erstwhile death grins at me in my cabin. Julia, the boatman's wife, knocks at the door and brings to me on my bier the morning drink of the country whose coasts we happen to be passing.' 'A terrible fate,' said the burgomaster, raising his hand defensively. 'And are you in any way to blame?' 'No,' said the hunter, 'I was a hunter, is there any sin in that? I was detailed to hunt in the Black Forest, where in those days there were still wolves. I used to lie in ambush, shoot, hit the mark and flay the skins, was that a sin? My labours were blessed. I was called the great hunter of the Black Forest. Is that a sin?' 'I am not competent to decide that,' said the burgomaster, 'but there seems no sin in it to me. But who then is to blame?' 'The boatman,' said the hunter. 'And now you intend to stay here with us in Riva?' asked the burgomaster. 'I do not,' said the hunter with a smile, and to excuse the jest he laid his hand on the burgomaster's knee. 'I am here, more than that I do not know. My boat has no rudder, it is driven by the wind that blows in the nethermost regions of death.'

BIOGRAPHICAL NOTE

Franz Kafka was born in Prague in 1883. His parents were Jewish, and his family spoke both Czech and German, Kafka attending German-speaking schools and training in law at university. He graduated in 1906, going on to work for the Workers' Accident Insurance Office, where his professional success was hindered only by his being diagnosed with tuberculosis of the larynx in 1917. In spite of time spent in various sanatoria, his health deteriorated further, obliging him to retire in 1922.

In his lifetime Kafka published one collection of stories (including *Metamorphosis*). It is due to his literary executor, the novelist and philosopher Max Brod, that, contrary to Kafka's request that his work be burnt after his death, his three novels (*The Trial*, 1925, *The Castle*, 1926, and *America*, 1927) were published. Further short fiction also appeared post-humously.

Kafka did much of his writing at night, yet despite this, and in contrast with his reputation as the creator of isolated protagonists in cold, confusing worlds, he in fact enjoyed a busy social life. His friends included the playwright Franz Werfel, and he also spent time swimming, hiking, and travelling. Emotionally, however, Kafka lived an unhappy life. The oppressive influence of his father dominated his other relationships; he never married, though he was twice engaged to Felice Bauer, and found a close companion in his final years in Dora Diamant. He died aged forty at a nursing home in Kierling near Vienna. His enormous stylistic influence and unique means of expressing perplexity, guilt, and loneliness in clear prose, has assured his critical reputation as one of the greatest European writers.

Richard Stokes teaches languages at Westminster School, coaches singers in the interpretation of Lieder, and gives frequent lectures on song composers. He has co-authored a number of books on German, French, and Spanish song, and his translations of Berg's *Wozzeck* (Opera North), Wagner's *Parsifal* and Berg's *Lulu* (both English National Opera) met with great acclaim.

HESPERUS PRESS – 100 PAGES

Hesperus Press, as suggested by the Latin motto, is committed to bringing near what is far – far both in space and time. Works written by the greatest authors, and unjustly neglected or simply little known in the English-speaking world, are made accessible through new translations and a completely fresh editorial approach. Through these short classic works, each little more than 100 pages in length, the reader will be introduced to the greatest writers from all times and all cultures.

For more information on Hesperus Press, please visit our website: **www.hesperuspress.com**

To place an order, please contact:
Grantham Book Services
Isaac Newton Way
Alma Park Industrial Estate
Grantham
Lincolnshire NG31 9SD
Tel: +44 (0) 1476 541080
Fax: +44 (0) 1476 541061
Email: orders@gbs.tbs-ltd.co.uk

SELECTED TITLES FROM HESPERUS PRESS

Gustave Flaubert *Memoirs of a Madman*

Alexander Pope *Scriblerus*

Ugo Foscolo *Last Letters of Jacopo Ortis*

Anton Chekhov *The Story of a Nobody*

Joseph von Eichendorff *Life of a Good-for-nothing*

Mark Twain *The Diary of Adam and Eve*

Giovanni Boccaccio *Life of Dante*

Victor Hugo *The Last Day of a Condemned Man*

Joseph Conrad *Heart of Darkness*

Edgar Allan Poe *Eureka*

Emile Zola *For a Night of Love*

Daniel Defoe *The King of Pirates*

Giacomo Leopardi *Thoughts*

Nikolai Gogol *The Squabble*

Herman Melville *The Enchanted Isles*

Leonardo da Vinci *Prophecies*

Charles Baudelaire *On Wine and Hashish*

William Makepeace Thackeray *Rebecca and Rowena*

Wilkie Collins *Who Killed Zebedee?*

Théophile Gautier *The Jinx*

Charles Dickens *The Haunted House*

Luigi Pirandello *Loveless Love*

Fyodor Dostoevsky *Poor People*

E.T.A. Hoffmann *Mademoiselle de Scudéri*

Henry James *In the Cage*

Francesco Petrarch *My Secret Book*

D.H. Lawrence *The Fox*

Percy Bysshe Shelley *Zastrozzi*